Reviews for previous work

First-rate, playful, moving.

– The Times

Elegant and even-handed biography.

– Wall Street Journal

A fascinating read.

– The Economist

An engrossing and intelligent portrait
of a man and an era.

– Evening Standard

As they say in the tour de France: chapeau!.

– Spectator

Passionate, risk-taking, aesthetically
conservative: a compendious biography.

– Guardian

A likeable, informative and poignant book.

– Literary Review

Hugely readable and well-researched.

– The Scotsman

THE QUEEN'S LENDER

LENDER

– A novel set in history

By

JEAN FINDLAY

Scotland Street Press
EDINBURGH

First Published in the UK in February 2022 by
Scotland Street Press
100 Willowbrae Avenue
Edinburgh EH8 7HU

Second Edition Published June 2022

A CIP record for this book is available from the British Library.

ISBN 978-1-910895-55-9

Typeset by Antonia Shack in Edinburgh
Cover Design by Antonia Shack
Cover image: Portrait of Anne of Denmark (1574-1619),
Unknown Artist (1595-1603), Oil on panel, 65.5 x 49.5 cm,
Government art collection, British Embassy, Copenhagen

Printed and bound by CPI Group (UK) Ltd, Croydon, CR0 4YY

For Alastair

Contents

One

Edinburgh, Scotland – 1593

A pregnant woman is a fragile being, and George has two on his hands: his wife, who keeps reminding him she is his queen, and his Queen who is in fact his queen. Queen Anna was a young bride: betrothed at thirteen, wed at fifteen, now pregnant at seventeen. She is a strong and healthy lass with ruddy hair and blossoming cheeks, an excited girlish laugh and a great love of rubies, which suit her beautifully.

George's hand shakes, not with tiredness or with fear, but with excitement, as he writes in his neat accounts book with his scratchy quill, 'twa hingeris fur luggies, with twa dossen rubies'. He will only charge her for the cost of the earrings, not the workmanship, which is good – the best; his father was King's Jeweller, and George learnt by watching his father's hands. But Anna is a joy to work for – no one has ever appreciated his jewellery with such abandon. And the King is indulgent – whatever she desires is hers, no matter what the cost. The price is never even mentioned.

Diamonds and emeralds arrive in pockets of weary traders, burnt by the sun and dirtied by the roads; not obvious bringers of fortune but disguised from the real thieves by looking like thieves themselves, and travelling more at ease since George's father's time, in a country more at peace.

George lifts his head as his wife enters. The first-floor room is rounded at the corner and lined with oak which keeps it warm. There is a small window looking out over the dark close.

'Thinkin aboot ma faither, agin, Christian.'

Christian stands for a moment, imagining her father-in-law, 'He ayeways looks me straight in the een.'

'Which is more than I can say fur his Grace, King James…'

'Why? Why is he like that, George? Jist Kingly?'

'Naw. If folk told ye from childhood that yer ain mither had murdered yer faither, that would punish the heart and soul.'

'And then they beheadit her, the Queen, his mither, the bonnie, bonnie Queen.'

'Then ye wouldna trust a' body.'

'Lady Marjorie cam' roon the day and said that there's a play in London aboot this, and set in Elsinore too, so we ken where the story comes fae. Aboot a Prince whose mither plots the death o his faither. But it's sweetened up.'

'Aye, all stories are sweetened up, tae mak life bearable.'

'I'm tired George, I'm awa tae bed.' She lifts the woollen wall-hanging with her left hand, caressing her stomach as she moves.

He has to stop blethering and finish these books. 'The accounts are what will bring you through,' he remembers his father saying, 'Brawness o' the jewel is important, but the patter is more so and most of all is the sums.' It is past midnight and the High Street is brisk with life. Shouts and laughter, the hum of warm and ribald talk in the tavern next door. A slice of fiddle music each time the door opens. George's home and workshop are in Fishmarket Close, a smelly wynd, but narrow and steep so the bones and guts from the fish shops will sluice downhill with the rain. It is clean now as he steps outside. A moment's hesitation – last year he would have entered the tavern. But now his wife is with child and a delicate person, desirous and deserving of attention. The sheer glory of the child within her envelops him, but instead of going to join his wife he charges back into the workshop.

A piece of beaten gold lies quivering on the end of his small hammer, precious like the stuff of life itself. Strange that he should expect a first child at the same time as the

King, whose baby will one day be King of Scotland *and* of England if word is to be believed at Court. That's the worry. So rushed and full of activity, can the Queen keep the child, child as she is herself? Bearing this baby who will be King. This film of beaten gold, so flimsy now, will outlast them all: the film of life within the womb, so dim and rare, might disappear in a giddy dance or a too tightly strung stay or the excitement of a gallop in the woods on her horse.

Queen Anna loves his bletherings, and courtiers notice that George in fact looks like, sounds like, is almost the same age as Anna's husband King James, but is a much gentler version, and one that listens. They both have reddish beards and blue eyes, but George's hair is lighter in colour, a soft strawberry blond, and there is less fear in his eyes than in those of James. He can afford to be open and direct in his gaze. He is altogether a kinder, more handsome version of James, and he does not have the strange almost-limp with a turned-out foot that James does his best to hide.

Anna can listen to George for ages and then order a jewel. But the jewels need discussion in great detail. Today it's a religious scene done in emerald and ruby with a pearl border. Here is the Wisdom of Solomon where King Solomon, faced with a custody dispute over a baby, orders the baby to be cut in half. Solomon knows that the real mother will do anything to stop her child being killed, even offer the baby to a stranger. One woman immediately offers the babe to the other and so Solomon sees at once she is the genuine mother. This moment of justice deserves picking out in gold and precious gems.

Pregnant Anna hates the story but knows that such questions of life and death over their subjects she and King James have to decide daily. James is the Solomon of Scotland. George sees this at once and launches into enthusiastic talk, so much that Anna gets her husband from his chamber to join the planning of the tiny scene, and so flattered and agreeable is James at the analogy, that he makes no fuss as to the cost,

'Whativer, dinna discuss the siller. Whit's important is the jewel at this time, when my Queen bears my heir, the future King o' Scotland and first king o' fower realms. Let it be done and snell.'

Anna interjects, 'But its no' a guid tale, a bairn been cut in half, a mither losing her bairn. I could nivver quit my ain child.'

James replies, 'But ye wid. To save a life, to protect yer ain child, ye wid.'

It is a sweet autumn day and the leaves are falling crisp on the dry ground. The mist is rising gently out of the Nor' Loch and George spies a red apple on a bough. Some people keep their back gardens well with apple trees – one day he will have an apple tree. In spite of the filth on the streets, or perhaps because of it, there are high-walled gardens behind the closes that lead off the way, and those who can grow fruit and vegetables have a constant gardener guarding them from many who are starving.

He walks out into the High Street and looks down hill: every morning the sea glints way below him. Such is the view looking down the Royal Mile. A fresh wind blows the sun in his face and an early fish-wife passes with a creel of herring on her back. He buys two and runs back down the Close to Christian – she appreciates that, and she kisses him, happy. There is time before his meeting with the Queen. Time to cook the herring and eat them together along with the small beer left over from the night before. He knows hot water is cleaner for breakfast, but small beer tastes better with herring, along with Christian's flat oatcakes baking warm on top of the stove. The light shines bright that morning on the dry oatcakes, on the blacked stove, on the shining herring skin and on his dear wife's clear skin, her infant blue eyes and light brown hair. Words are too much, her looks say it all: all love, all hope, all thankfulness. He knows he is a blessed man. It is early autumn, the driest, warmest, most fruitful October he has ever known.

Two

The Queen Bee

Lady Marjorie Boswell, sister-in-law to George's wife, is a force to be reckoned with: flame haired and well-bosomed, she doesn't look her forty-one years. She lives, like a queen bee, off the labour of others. The only sister of seven brothers, it is said she has engineered the divorces of two of them. She informed Peter, the elder, that his wife had taken a lover, and then he put her away for adultery. Now Marjorie commands Peter; he helps her with advice and money. She took his children under her care, but that was advisable as his eldest son is the heir to Connachie Castle and it means Marjorie and her brood could move into the family home where she herself grew up. She can't bear to have another woman around her and when Calum, her third brother, declared that his wife kept having still births and had sunk into a terrible melancholia, Marjorie advised having her put into an asylum. She does not reckon on Calum getting a younger, stronger, braver wife, but that is for the future. For the present Calum moves into Connachie Castle with Peter and his children, Marjorie and her family and it makes for a strong clan. Only women know how to build the clan. It is like a hive and needs workers, loyal men, brothers. They work and bring home the money, or honey as she prefers to call it.

Peter runs the farms, Calum helps. Marjorie's husband is a good book-keeper, and nine children, all cousins, run in and out of the courtyard taking lessons with their tutor, learning plants in the walled garden, riding with a good stable of horses and hunting with neighbouring gentry. Thirteen people are employed in and around the castle; overseeing them keeps Marjorie busy, and she's a very good if ruthless manager, which means she has plenty time to be present at Court in Edinburgh, close to power.

George Heriot knows her, he knows she likes young men and he manages so long as he flatters her, but he won't let his wife Christian near her, even though they are related by marriage: Marjorie has a crushing if not crunching effect on younger women. On a visit last year to Connachie Castle George couldn't find her inside the hall and went below to the kitchens in search, then out into the yard where the chickens are running loose in the mud and straw. There

Lady Marjorie rounds a corner and comes face to face with him, clutching in her right hand the feet of a decapitated cockerel, holding it aloft so that the blood doesn't spatter her skirts. In her left hand is a small axe. George notes first that she is left-handed, before she beams triumphantly,

'Too many cocks! Just like at court. And the new lassie has niver killed one hersel'. Here, take that inside, it's for our supper the night.' Then turning to the new servant, 'Look ye hauld the heid doon on the block and …' She whacks the tree stump chopping block with clear enjoyment. 'There.' She follows George into the kitchen and washes her hands in a basin of water. Her clothes are clean.

George is wise beyond his years. Working with metal and stones helps him slow down to the speed of feelings. The in-law relationship is a poisonous one, most often; the mother-in-law is difficult, the sister-in-law is difficult, the brother-in-law is difficult. The father-in-law is less difficult: George is not sure why, perhaps because his own is dead.

George sees the in-law relationship as naturally venomous, like the human body rejecting a foreign object – woe betide someone who comes home with a French wife – or an arrow head in the leg; the body will naturally reject it. A family will reject all its in-laws unless it makes a conscious daily decision to be Christian – and his wife Christian lives up to her name, but Lady Marjorie does not. Kinship binds, but jealousy simmers.

Arriving at Holyrood Palace and ushered into the royal presence, he is not surprised to see Lady Marjorie already ensconced in the small chamber, warmed by a good fire, lined with carved oak from Flanders, hung with French tapestries. This room was the favourite of the King's mother, Queen Mary, now dead, beheaded after a life in prison. But a Queen's life is always a life of prison, George thinks, looking at Queen Anna, so young, surrounded by the clever and the wise, the cunning and the ambitious.

Older women of the court, he notices, wear many large rings, larger and more numerous as they age. It is evidence of wealth, and distraction from a face that was once their attraction, to the more concrete assets of money and a good marriage. Lady Marjorie's hands are weighed down with silver. However, George does not work in silver much and does not want Lady Marjorie as a customer.

Lady Marjorie leans towards the Queen as George enters and whispers something about him. Anna beckons him forward and says hesitantly, 'I hear your wife is wi child, George. Ye maun bring her here tae be prisentit at court.'

George knows that Queen Anna has not composed that suggestion, she has no interest in his wife. He replies, 'All in guid time, your Grace, at present she's abed.'

Fortunately, her condition means she will be 'abed' for some time. He says nothing more, not wanting to discuss his work with Lady Marjorie present, not wanting to discuss anything with Lady Marjorie present, knowing that any knowledge of his affairs gives her ammunition for future danger. For a queen bee must not only succeed as herself, she must arrange that other women fail.

Queen Anna is not a bee, she is a real Queen and does not need to behave in this way. George believes she is above such dealings and hopes Lady Marjorie will have no influence.

As he leaves the Palace, an autumn leaf brushes his head and death brushes his cheek.

Three

Witches of the North

Death is all around in Edinburgh that year. It stalks the streets in the early hours and there are theories from the learned as to why.

The King, not only there by divine will, is also quite a sage himself, with ideas about the origins of such assaults of Satan. Witches, he believes, as do the men who surround him, are slaves of the Devil; they make a pact with Satan by eating his food and go on to curse ships.

The ship that brought James and his Queen Anna from Denmark just after their marriage was rocked by terrible storms they said caused by witches jumping up the keel the night before. It had been proven without doubt by his royal Danish in-laws and they had executed the witches.

James, convinced that Danish witches were in league with Scottish witches through Satan, has decided he will hunt them down.

The King's investigators discover witches nearby in Tranent, Haddington, Garvald and North Berwick, all places within a day's ride of Holyrood Palace. It is suspicious that they are all within a day's ride, of course, but the King's men do their job punctually and get results fast. And what is more satisfying than to meet and interrogate a witch in person?

James has Agnes Sampson brought to Holyrood where she is chained to a wall and then tortured to exact a confession. She claims to be a midwife and healer, a wise, elderly woman of the village, needed by all for her skills and service, however it is discovered through interrogation that she is in fact in league with the Devil, that she has caused the storms along with the Danish witches, that she can transform herself into a fish or a whale and cross the seas. Of course, she denies these accusations at first, but skilled examination, shaving, and head-wrenching always bring confessions in a weak woman.

***

At Elsinore in Denmark, two years before, after James and Anna were wed, there was a first attempt to return to Scotland, but storms prevented it. So there was a witch burning. Two women were found guilty by court of raising storms that would threaten the safety of royal ships, often and again, the same spells causing storms that wreck ships in that sea-going nation, for what else causes storms but spells? Even as a child Anna did not follow that logic.

Anna watched through a window inside Elsinore Castle: not near enough for detail, but with the imagination of a girl she did not need to be close to see the flames starting at the young womens' feet, catching the dress, the look of pain, horror, resignation, as the skin on legs and thighs blistered and melted, and the screams were torn from the exhausted girls. They had already been tortured to a state of subjugation, but not too far the torturer knew, so as not to spoil the spectacle of burning.

Anna had turned away towards her mother, but the faces of the young women were in her mind and she asked in agony, 'Why?'

'Evil women. If we don't get them, they will get us. These already plotted death by sea for you with your husband. All we need for evil to win is for good to do nothing,' explained Anna's father.

Anna turned to look at her future husband and saw a flicker of a smile, not of cruelty or sadism but of satisfaction at seeing justice done.

The King of Denmark was in the vanguard of witch hunters. He had theologians at Court trained in tracing demonology. The foremost, Tygore Delson, had an extended debate with James in Latin. No other royal could keep pace with the mind of the foremost intellectual in Copenhagen. Anna's heart beat faster when she heard how impressed her father was with the mind of his new son-in-law.

***

And now in Scotland James can go further, he knows he can discern a witch. King James is on the side of God and he will tackle the Devil directly. The people know him as the only King brave enough to take on the Devil himself. Other kings have gone to war to impress their subjects, but James goes straight to the perpetrator of absolute evil. He executes at source.

No wonder Anna loves the jewels. What sparkles with more innocence than a diamond, more purity than a pearl? And this particular scene, the scene of Solomon, unites James' love of the Bible with Anna's love of gems. It's so important that George is summoned to Stirling Castle to discuss the final details.

'Pearls o'er a border, your Grace,' proposes George,

'Like the pearly gates.' James agrees.

'Solomon's cloak in rubies.'

'How will ye dae the face?'

'Enamel. A method from Flanders: meltit glass on gold, and ye can paint as fine as a single bristle.'

'An' backit wi green.'

'Aaaooh…'

The men turn towards Anna. She is in pain; this first time hearing a convivial talk with George, her favourite courtier, and James her husband gives her such pleasure that her stomach hurts. A lady is called and Anna taken to sit down, then to lie down.

The pains continue and her lady orders the midwife.

The pain comes more persistently. Into Anna's mind floats the image of two women on a pyre in Copenhagen being burned. She opens her mouth, squeezes her eyes, crumples her forehead, and lets out a roar.

James hears Anna roar. He stops the jewel commission and demands an entrance. Other courtiers arrive, an audience to witness the Queen's agony and ensure any heir is the real thing, not a switchling.

The audience gets comfortable, they sit and order food, they chat, waiting for the show to begin. Anna knows how the witches felt, each shout of pain is part of the expected theatricals. Her father had a theatre built in each Danish palace, starting with Elsinore, and appointed a court playwright whose job it was to entertain with a different play every month, for which he had musicians. The courtiers were blasé about the shows, but she loved them. These Scots courtiers know few theatricals, their main entertainment is a death or a birth, and they are blasé about both.

Through gritted teeth she hates the smiles on the faces of the young men. There is sympathy among the women. Margaret holds her hand and whispers in her ear and the midwife strokes her feet. Kept so royal and pure above the hoi polloi, she is suddenly expected to spread her legs before an audience of men, some who leer. But each time the pain shoots through she does not care. This is like a death and it does not matter.

Prince Henry comes squealing into the world after an interminable night and Anna finds to her surprise that she is still alive. The audience leaves with her child and she is washed by Margaret and the energetic midwife, to whom she knows she owes her life. She sleeps, fervently hoping that this midwife, who has skillfully saved her from certain death, will not be accused of being a witch.

Four

Guilt

Guilt lies heavy upon George, like a thick woollen coverlet that has gone damp in an old house. Every time his mother speaks about he and Christian not visiting, he falls sad. Each step towards his wife is a betrayal of his mother and each step towards his mother a betrayal of his wife. That afternoon, with George back from Stirling Castle, his mother arrives, bent under her shawl and walking painfully.

'I shouldna have to travel tae visit a healthy son,' she jokes knocking her walking stick against George's leg. 'A'm no' sae far away.'

'I hae muckle wark, mither.'

'And that's a' guid, wi a wean on the way, but dinna forget your family noo ye hae a fancy life being the Queen's jeweller.'

It has been announced that George would be made First Deacon of Goldsmiths. At such a young age this is unusual and other and better jewellers are jealous. They say he has the Queen's ear, some say he has more than her ear. He can relax, not tout for work at the end of every commission. King James understands this about a life – he has his faults, but he's the cleverest king in Christendom. Who else speaks so many languages? James spoke Latin and Greek before he spoke Scots, French of course because of his mother, his grandmother and the Auld Alliance, now German and Danish, picked up at the Danish Court. Once one language is learnt, the others come easily to a tutored young mind. Queen Anna tells George all of this, she's forever proud of how brilliant her husband is. True, she now spends more time with George than with James, but maybe that will change with the birth of a son.

'Ah'm here tae hear aboot it, son,' says his mother eagerly. 'Were ye there for the birth?'

'I didnae, couldnae…'

'Whit, ye had tickets for the best show in town, in the country, in all Europe and ye gibbered out?'

'There was a gey big crowd.'

'It's your preevilege. What's the title King's Jeweller fur then?'

'It's fur makin' jewels for King and Queen the best I can, no' watching a birth. I'll hae my own birth soon enough.'

'Ye could hae learnt some.'

Christian speaks from the corner of the room quietly. 'I am glad you didnae watch George, ye're more a man for it. But... I hope ye'll stay for our ane child.'

George goes to Christian to take her hand tenderly, 'There'll no' be the same crowd. Only the midwife and oorselves.'

'Naw,' says his mother excitedly, 'I'm no going to miss this ane. Guid and weel, I'm stayin'. I'm sleepin here the nicht, ye'll need me ower soon.' She rises painfully and crookedly, 'We'll hae a cauldron o water boilin' just in case.'

Christian looks frightened.

George is wary of his mother's thirst for drama. 'Why?'

'Ye ayways need boilin' water at a birth, ye dafties. The midwife will tell ye. There's much tae clean.'

Christian has not so far seen the birth of their child as a cleaning exercise. She is silent, thinking her thoughts and holding the hand of the husband she adores. She stands and holds him.

Old Mrs Heriot snorts – 'O aye, keep doing that and the bairn will come soon enough.'

Her comment stops them at once.

George takes up his apron, which keeps his tools folded in the pockets, and excuses himself for the workshop.

The workshop is close and dark like a womb. It smells of hot metal and stone. All the familiar tools lie on the bench as he lights his candles. Daylight is best for intricate work and the window seat holds his tiny markers, with a clean linen cloth laid out to catch any pieces of precious metal or gem. Emeralds are always the dearest, the rarest and the bonniest. They come from lands afar and the traders would tell his father of their travels to hot countries on foot, on horse or camel. George likes to think of the heat as he polishes the green gem with infinite care, his fingers strong and slim, blackened in the cracks with metal work, his nails short, no rings on him, none at all. Hands are for work, not decoration. When you cut a stone, it is not really a cut, more a graze, a filing, and it has to land on the right place, so a minute flat face can be shown which twinkles in the right light and the right light is either sunlight, the best, or a single candle flame which gives a dark deep insight into the stone itself. And in there lies a mystery. He can stare at an uncut diamond for hours before doing anything, before knowing where it needs a face; the more he looks the further he can see. Gem watching is his pleasure; not the acquisition, but the working of a stone.

For Anna it is the acquiring, he knows that. They share a love of jewels, but their love has different approaches. George's love is not possessive, and in that sense it is a true love; he wants the best cut for the stone, he knows the best cut, like a wise woman advising her grandchildren on their future.

That thought brings him back to his mother, waiting for another grandchild with all the impatience of expectation.

Yet he is glad she is there, so much can go wrong. And the words of his Queen just not long before she gave birth ring in his head:

'Creating another human soul is the maist powerful thing a body can iver do, which is why man will niver surpass women,' the teenage Anna says to him, in the company of her ladies.

'Yet we are a' taught that womankind is lesser,' George replies.

'Niver. Creation o' children is god-like. You just mak things, rings, and such like. Try makin a child!'

All the anger in that strange, decorated indoor flower, that Queen of his, comes out in the vehemence of success. Her beauty now is mesmerizing, something vivid no painter can catch. A live child, a Prince Henry. She made him and she knows it. But can she keep him?

Birdsong gladdens the heart, and spring though slow, does arrive for George and Christian and with it the promise of new life. It is till May, only a promise, but the round, swelling belly of his loved wife gives George a hope in the future he's never held so strongly before. Her skirts burst with the child within. She is shy and surprised at her size and does not want to go out. George takes to walking with her in the evening past the gardens and into the Palace grounds, which are heavy with blossom and the cut grass dotted with white and yellow flowers. The mound of

Arthur's Seat rises beside them as daunting to Christian as her own round form, but they do not climb it as they have done before. He points to Saint Anthony's chapel,

'Under it in a crag tae the left is a cave where ye can bide but still see Edinburgh. Dry and warm, ye'll spy boats docking in Leith, see the Kingdom o' Fife – and even right intae Holyrood Palace. A man in that cave can see us here in the gairdens.'

All is seen, all is known. They are all being watched.

Once in the Palace grounds they see Lady Marjorie leave and hang back lest she spies them. George pulls at Christian's arm and stops her while they both watch Lady Marjorie speak to the coachman, then stare sharply as another gentlewoman entered the palace. Marjorie has, thinks George, a striking face, but the look of a woman who has aged without maturing. She competes with all women. As soon as she meets a possible contender, she is determined to be above her in beauty, fashion, wealth and class. She will manipulate others to achieve this. She has worked her way into the highest echelons of Court and that, he has to admit, is useful.

Nonetheless, people will always be fascinated by breeding and while Lady Marjorie is an aristocrat, George is not. Her son James meets George the next morning on the steps of Fishmarket Close and says,

'I heard ye wantit a horse. I hae Pricker here.'

'I dinna want a horse,'

'Have ye no seen him on the flat? I'll tak' him down for ye.'

'I dinna need a horse.'

'Every gentleman needs a horse. Do you niver cross the Nor Loch? Iver go tae Leith?'

The trees are bulky like great bushes beneath them and the Nor Loch is deep.

'I walk to work,'

'No tae Stirling Castle ye don't. Ye borrowed ma faither's. Buy yin o' yer ain.'

'I hae no stabling.'

'Stablin's no trouble in Embra toon. Ye can rent it nearby.'

This is the eldest son of Lady Marjorie and trained or influenced by her persistent manner, her lack of tact, never to take no for an answer.

'I dinna want nor need a horse. I'm happy tae borrow or hire. Here. That's fur the hire o your faither's horse forbye.'

'It's ower much. But I'll tak it. Thank you.'

The seagulls are screaming to each other in the close, reminding him of the latest fearful story of a great ship that went down with all on board drowned.

'I dinna need tae gang tae Leith,' George states.

He turns up the High Street to visit David Brown. David is a noted corn-operator but not a seller of grain, he is a dentist and a chiropodist, and is writing a learned document on the removal of corns. Since the fashion of high wooden heels at Court, David is much in demand. But George does not get to the end of his close,

'Wir spoiled wi this weather, urnt wi?'

His mother is back: on good form.

'And tae think that aince ye sookled at ma briest.'

The idea makes George wince. Suckling at breasts is for younger folk. His ancient mother is nearly fifty-eight and few women live that long. She still has some of her teeth, though not the front two, and she can walk well enough with a stick, which she also uses to great effect in conversation.

'Oot o' ma road, ye shoogly.'

A man on a horse is attempting to make his way up the close, only to encounter George's mother, to his and his horse's great fright. The animal rears after being struck by her stick and throws its rider into some deep sludge in the corner of the alley.

'George, Maister Heriot,' pleads the rider rising, covered in foul smelling mud, setting his jewelled bonnet back on his head.

Mrs Heriot has hooked the bridle expertly with her stick and hands the horse over to her son.

'There's nae room fur beasts up a close,' she announces and rattles back up the hill towards the High Street.

The rider turns out to be Lord Lennox. He has heard about the buttons recently designed for the King's jacket and wants some for himself, to appear only the day after the King wears them in public.

'Why?' is the first question in George's head, but he is wise enough not to voice every thought.

'Come awa' in.' He ties the horse.

His workshop is tiny but pleasant and always warm because of the small forge that melts his metals.

Lennox sits, 'Buttons fae the padded court jerkin, a topaz in the middle tae match my een and each one surroundit wi pearls, no, twa rows o' pearls.'

George looks into Lennox's topaz eyes, and at his reddish beard, immaculately coiffed, and his filthy cloak, and adopts his detached tone for business.

'Topaz and pearls, they arnae the dearest, but they cost. An' the metal base? Siller is best ... I'll hae to charge ye in advance, tae find the gems, tae buy the gems, tae wark the gems ... I'll need a dossan grand topaz and fourteen wee pearls fir each ...'

'And cuffs, I'll hae four on each cuff,' adds his eager and valued customer.

George charges twice the amount that he did for the King's, and all in advance.

Lennox doesn't flinch; on top he asks that the jewels be unique, unique to him and the King alone, that Heriot must make them for no one else. George charges him a premium for this uniqueness. Lennox pays at once in merks; he is in a hurry to be away with his horse and his dirty cloak.

That evening Christian watches as George writes up the order in his ledger, the description, cost, timings and advance. He counts the money again and locks it in a drawer.

'Noo I can afford tae mak things for the Queen.'

'How's so?' Asks his wife.

I dinna charge for the wark wi' the Queen, sometimes I dinna charge for the jewels. No at first, anyway. I record it for the Chancellor, he's the man that maun pay, and he's guid. Writes it a' doon.'

'But you record it too?'

'Aye, it's here in the books. Ye must ken that, Christian, should ever a' thing happen to me. A' that's owed me is in the books. Wealth is foondit on trust, trust and weil-kept buiks.'

Christian does not show her disapproval of Lennox and his like, but it is evident in her expression, 'And mibbe fin' a way o' movin all the merks frae the rich folk wha dinna need it, to the puir folks wha do.'

Heriot realises his luck, 'Guid wife, a noble thocht.' A sudden fear grips him, born of acute love for Christian, a terror of losing her, as so many men lose their young wives to childbirth or illness. 'My best, my bonniest and my dearest.' He stands and holds her close.

Five

Ambassadors and spies

Not everyone will lie in order to please someone else, but diplomats will; it is firstly their nature and secondly their job. Don d'Aragno bows low before King James and declares that the jewel of King Solomon's Judgment is the most outstanding he has seen anywhere in all the courts of Europe. James is mightily pleased. The Don continues that Their Graces have excessively good taste and can vie with the greatest European powers in patronage of the arts. He has visited many courts and can vouch for it.

Now he cuts straight to the point.

He hopes that James will exercise similar wisdom in judgment over the question of an Alliance with Spain in order to conquer the English and by force, put James himself on the throne of England and organize a marriage for young Henry with a Spanish Princess.

James arches his eyebrow,

'My new laddie is ower young to think o' matches wi' princesses.'

That is a card he can keep till later on.

Anna interrupts, 'Straight after birth, we dinna want war – certain death for mony men. Women gie birth and menfolk kill.'

She bursts into tears and is taken away by her Danish Margaret.

James puts the jewel on his bonnet again. It is definitely a hat jewel fit only for a king; and exercising Solomonic judgement, he answers the Spanish nobleman.

'As for my title to the Crown of England, after my cousin's decease, which thing if she grant it, we will hae attained oor desire wi'oot stroke o' sword.'

The perfect answer.

And it is heard by enough courtiers so that he can be sure that it will be relayed to Elizabeth without him lifting a finger. He can rely on her spies at court. And he has not even insulted his esteemed guest.

'Don D'Aragno will ye jyne us the morn for a hunt in Holyrood Park? Tis walled and safe and full o' tame deer.'

The Spaniard is put out, 'I will be honoured to join your Grace, but I can hunt wild deer.'

James is laughing as he goes to see Anna in her chamber.

'Are you going tae war?' she asks from the bed, steadily. Margaret is at her side with cold cloths for her brow. The room smells of lavender and sage oils and the good Danish woman has calmed her Queen.

She is indeed beautiful. James takes the jewel from his bonnet and sets it in her headdress.

'There is nae need for war, nae war. The answer is naw.'

Anna smiles up at him, fingering the jewel.

James glances at her propped up against the bedstead, and quotes, 'Thy twa briests are like twa young roes whae are twins, that feed amang the lilies.'

Anna, not knowing it as his own translation from Solomon's Song, starts again to weep, silently. 'Please let me see my child. My bairnie. My briests long for my child.'

James stands up in martial pose. 'The Prince Henry will stay with the Earl o' Mar, as I did, till he is of age. He needs instruction an' safe-keepin. No-one is tae enter Stirling Castle sauf they on the list.'

Margaret intervenes, curtseying, 'At Elsinore the Princes are guardit at Court, where guards are vigilant and love is near.'

James paces. 'My gracious Queen hae borne oor heir and all Scotland rejices. But Scotland isnae Denmark, and rebels abound. Not a year sine I had it declared fae the pulpit to squash the vile rumours spread by oor enemies, three things – James isnae son of Riccio, but rightful King.

James did consummate his marriage.' His voice rising to a shout, 'James isnae a bugger.'

He was pacing the room by this time.

'My Queen has provit thus by deliverin safely oor Prince Henry. But we still have enemies, those who wish us ill, and Henry will be guardit and educatit safely as I wis at Stirling Castle by the Earl and Countess o' Mar. Nane shall be permittit to enter the Castle save those on the list. In the security of my son consists my ain and oor security.'

His voice rises again as he finishes and leaves the room.

***

Meanwhile not far from the Palace, with George and Christian Heriot, there is also a giving-over of jewels, just for viewing, not for keeps. Christian loves the glisten of a diamond well cut by her husband and admires his work while she busies herself in preparation for the birth of their child. She has stopped walking with George in the evening to the Palace, alarmed as she is by his awareness that they are all being watched. Alarm gives her fear for their child. She makes blankets and sews linen for a new-born. George brings in a serving girl who helps in the house and he gets an apprentice for his workshop next door in the close.

The eve of the birth is dark and wet, and Christian is by turns hot and then shivering with cold. Old Mrs Heriot is not, as she has planned, at home with her son. The cauldron of water is not prepared, and the young maid is feart for her mistress who seems not herself, and not anyone else either. Mary, the maid, at length knocks on the door of George's workshop, standing in the rain.

'Come, the Mistress needs help, I'm feart for her.'

George instantly runs inside, only to behold a scene of agony he cannot understand. He runs up the High Street to his friend Mr Brown, the corn operator.

'You're a man o' science, come see efter my wife.'

'No, no, I cannae dae this, George, go and find a midwife', says the shy and unmarried Brown.

The midwife is attached to the Palace, and George has spoken with her before and arranged that she might help if needed. He runs downhill and is at the gate in five minutes, where his friends let him in and at once to the serving quarters. The midwife is with the Queen, the Queen is with Lady Marjorie. They are closeted inside the Audience chamber, the small but beautiful room decorated by the King's mother and with the arms of his French grandmother carved on the ceiling.

Outside the door stands a guard: a youth told that on no account should anyone enter.

You do not need to engineer a death in these times. All you need do is delay the midwife.

'Whit does Lady Marjorie hae agin me?'

'Naethin George, but yer wife may become favourt by the Queen, yer son may become favourt by the King, and Lady Marjorie disnae want folk in her way.' George is not sure if the voice is inside his head or from the guard.

If he were another man, a Bothwell, a man of passion, he would take on the guard and hammer the door and kick his way in to demand the midwife and plead with his Queen. But George is a circumspect courtier, a deferential and respectful servitor. He knows that Bothwell is now banished from Scotland for the hurly burly he committed at the Palace not long ago. It is always wise to control the passion no matter how grave.

There must be another woman who knows a bit of birthing. He asks the cook from the kitchen, but she cannot be spared. Then he begs the serving lass, the laundry maid.

She runs with George up the street in the rain and in through the Canons' Gait after more prevarications with the Porter and a hand over of coins.

At last they reach Christian, in bed and failing: the child not born, but stuck: the maid Mary distraught. The palace laundry maid, Ruth, is practical.

'Bile water, Mary! Bring cloths. Now a cold one, on the forehead. You'll be fine Mistress Heriot, just breath nice and slow. Water tae drink, Mary! Awa ye go Mister Heriot, this is no' for the likes o' you.'

George sits with his gems till daylight filters through the rain.

'How are you the morn Mister Heriot? Up early?' asks the fishwife.

He raises his head from his workbench and realizes slowly that no one has called him. Staggering towards the kitchen door, he hears crying within, but not a child's cry. It is the sobbing of women. Mary and Christian are weeping over the small, still bundle in his wife's arms. Ruth, sleeves up, arms stained with blood comes towards him.

'I couldna save the bairn, Mister Heriot, but your wife is well. She's here and mony a wummin dies wi' the baby hurdie ways roon as he wis.'

'He?'

'Aye, a laddie. But she's young and well, she'll hae another.'

Ruth's ruddy optimism stalls George again.

'Hurdie ways?'

'Aye. The heid should come furst wi' a birthing, no' the hurdies.'

'Witchcraft,' Says Mary from the bedside.

'There's nae sic thing,' retorts Ruth. 'It's just a still birth.'

'It would hae happened onyway?' asks George.

'Early times a guid wife can turn a bairn in the womb, but she maun be early.'

'Thank you, Ruth. Tak this for your pains.'

'I wish I could gie you something for your ain, Mister Heriot.'

As Ruth leaves, George kneels by the side of Christian and slowly takes the dead child from her. He kisses her as she falls back exhausted, and then stands to examine the small corpse in his arms.

'A proper burial,' he promises, laying it on a blanket in the hallway, but has to get out in the fresh air.

Once outside, George howls silently, grief tearing at him. He can't see properly because of his tears. As he blunders across the uneven cobbles his feet slip on the new mud and he holds onto the nearby wall for balance. He feels like dashing his head against it. That would solve things. Then he wouldn't feel any more and there would be no more pain.

But a close is not a private place and his neighbour Jessie comes up behind kindly putting a hand on his shoulder.

'A dram will help ye, Dod, a dram and a smoke.'

George does not drink or smoke and hates being called Dod, but the mellow compassion of the woman stops him cracking his forehead on the ancient stone wall.

What's more he gulps her whisky and smokes her pipe and feels differently.

'Have ye always smokit a pipe, Jessie?'

'Ever sin I could afford tae,' replies Jessie, 'it's a braw pipe, a' wood. No like the clay yins.'

Anything to stop the frantic beating in his head and heart. He draws the rancid smoke into his lungs, swallows and chokes, coughing spittle and making Jessie laugh.

Six

A pelican of the wilderness, an owl of the desert

Psalm 102 is a prayer of the afflicted where the supplicant pours out his soul to God, and this is what George reads to Christian on the burial day. It is the only copy of a new translation, it is rumoured by the King himself, and it is handed over to George, by order of the Queen.

'I am like a pelican o' the wilderness, I am like an owl o' the desert.' Christian repeats the line. 'What is a pelican?'

'Must be a great bird like an owl or an eagle, a lonely bird, a craitur alone on its jurney throu life, standin' afore God with nae comfort.'

'We hae comfort.'

'Aye, but sorrow visits us in solitude.'

'Tell Mary to wheesht wi' her lies of witches.'

'She'll be put oot the door, if she doesn't.'

Hearing what her masters say, Mary never utters another word about witchcraft.

She hears of course of the witches dunked in the Nor Loch below, but they never return, and they drown, which was proof of their evil. But she does not mention them again in the company of her master and mistress lest she lose her job. There is much evil that goes on in the streets that she does not mention to Christian, right outside their own door there are hawkers and whores and thieves and brigands. But now she will shield her mistress more, poor soul, and cheer her up. She will try and look happy sometimes.

A week later, 'An Owl in the Desert' is the subject of the sampler Christian is sewing. Embroidered in green silk thread on pale linen. Mary finds some red silk and brings it to her mistress,

'To mak' the owl look merry like. He might be smilin'

Christian puts her right, 'Owls dinna smile. We folk smile, but owls are serious craiters, they behaud the Almighty.'

George himself is pale and serious when summoned before his King and instructed to create a jewel as a gift to the Queen for the birth of their son and heir,

'Ayeways to please the Queen, because she needs pleasin. She wants tae tend Prince Henry and that isnae leasome. He will be guardit and nourishit in the ways o' a King.'

For this placatory gift, he suggests the most extravagant gems.

'Emeralds and diamonds … na, rubies!'

George takes orders with deference but without joy.

Queen Anna is more sensitive. She asks after Christian, and George tells of their sorrow. 'Your son may not be wi' you, your Grace, but at least he bides on this earth.'

The Queen is not happy with this reply,

'To think o' others worse off niver heals the hairt,' she says.

'Then perhaps a dozen rubies can be a balm. Look intae the gemstone an see a thousand lichts o' warmth.'

He holds a sample before the Queen and she, mesmerised, takes the ruby and stares, moving it into the sunlight by the open window.

'If I dropped it…' she utters playfully.

George moves to her fast.

'I'd rather visit my ain son than hae a hunner o' these. Just a visit. Can ye lend me the siller for the jurney?'

'How?'

'Pawn this. Let his Grace think you are warkin on it. Gie me glass, or enamel. He willna notice.'

George pauses. Never before would he consider deluding his King. But to help his Queen visit her son from whom she is banished… He owes his loyalty to both, but he is in the presence of the Queen, and in spite of himself, he feels more than loyalty or duty, but a desire to protect and shield from hurt. What can hurt more than the loss of your own child?

He agrees.

The Queen assembles her ladies and their horses and the garments they need for the visit. Those that are feart of the King's wrath they leave behind. The King is away on a week-long hunting trip when Anna sets out with her small entourage and packed horses, a few grooms and some loyal men to show the way. Stirling is only a day's ride distance, but the rain is heavy, the roads steeped in mud, and the sky a glowering grey, thick with mist.

'Your Grace, please wait a day. The haar will lift, the rains stop.'

She will not wait.

'You are mair use tae your son in guid health, your Grace, not wracked wi' coughin or fevers.'

At the moment she is no use at all to her son. Superfluous. Excess to requirements. What does it matter, a wet cloak?

Anna leaves with her retinue and the two hundred pounds forwarded to her by Heriot. The rain clears as they travel west. Anna's thick woollen cloak with fur lining provides ample protection though it smells of damp animal by the time they enter the hall at Stirling Castle. All know she is there without permission from the King, against his orders and against the rules of the Castle, but who can forbid their Queen to see her own child?

'Your brave and splendent Grace honours us wi' a brief visit,' says the elder Countess of Mar as Anna enters. The Countess manages to flatter, welcome, but lay down the rules in one short statement.

After a lengthy meal, the Queen asks to see her child and is ushered into the nursery. Needless to say, the baby does not recognize his mother but clings to the wet-nurse who suckles him. She hands over the baby who cries loud at once and poor Anna, totally ignorant of childrearing, hands him back. She stays near him as long as she can, watching as the servants nurse him and cuddle him and rock him to sleep. Then Anna admires Henry and strokes his little hands and cheeks.

'Has her Grace washit her hauns?'

The Countess of Mar makes the young mother jolt.

'I can see you keep him well,' says the Queen as they all curtsy before her, including the Countess.

'I hope your visit finally puts your mind at rest o'er that, your Grace.' Adds the Countess. 'Finally' is given a French emphasis, which she corrects in Scots.

'Enfin, Finalement et Lastlins, your Grace.'

Seven

Edinburgh 1599 – The work
of a cunning workman

Frost burns the grass outside. The last delicate serving of autumn is November: leaves still intact but few on the branches. Berries still brighten the eye and the birds still feast. Yew berries are delicious to behold but poisonous to swallow and small vomits of brown, filled with bright red fruits, from animals unknown to George, splatter the paths around the Palace gardens, like gemstones sitting next to the crisping leaves.

Old Mrs Heriot explains to Christian about the yew berries.

'Touch not the yew.'

'It looks so like the haw bush, but has nae thorns. Easier tae pick.'

'Haw berries mak a guid jam. But not the yew. Niver eat the seeds, for it is the seed o' the yew that causes death to bird, beast or man within three days.'

George's mother, though occasionally coarse, is a fount of wisdom on foodstuffs. She prepared victuals for the healing of Christian's mind and body after the death of her child and now four years later a son is born who thrives and suckles a wet-nurse, affordable now by the Queen's able jeweller, declared Queen's jeweller for life by trumpet at the Mercat Cross. They acquire more rooms for their house in Fishmarket Close and the nursemaid resides within. Christian wanted to feed the bairn herself but George forbade it, as becoming of his growing station in life and advised by his mother,

'Ye dinna wish her tae become like me.'

George is puzzled, but does not want Christian to age that fast. His mother continues,

'There's a lot tae me as no been seen. An when I die, a' the sins will come runnin aff me like rats aff a sinking ship.'

Rats? Death? He engages a wet-nurse at once. This time Ruth the laundry maid from the Palace arranges one. There have been six nurses coming forward for a job at the Palace because the Queen has given birth to two girls in the intervening years, Princess Elizabeth and Princess Margaret. Elizabeth is three and Margaret nearly a year, but still needing a wet-nurse. The Queen is happy as the girls, being mere girls, are allowed to stay fifteen miles away in the Palace of Linlithgow and Anna can see them at times. She speaks to the wet-nurses herself and knows the woman who is passed on to George and Christian.

'My mither talks o' death and sin so much praisently.' George confesses to Anna, on the occasion of a new jewel design and new funds to be lent. For George is more than the Queen's jeweller, he has become their Graces' money lender and pawnbroker.

George, diffident as he is and canny, has become a favourite, along with his jewels. But these not only embellish the Queen; she also uses his jewels as gifts for foreign ambassadors. Rings are small nuggets of wealth that can be easily carried away as favours for alliances in Europe. Heriot's designs are by now scattered over the continent.

Anna has no idea of the value of money or the cost of living. She came from a rich Danish Empire to a king who adores her. Why shouldn't she have everything she wants? Now she has two little princesses, to be adorned as richly as their mother, and each gift requires a visit.

George is walking in Holyrood Park. The last of the wet leaves have fallen from the trees like fragile clothing, just wasted in piles, ignored. If they were real, old Mrs Heriot would fold, wash, iron and mend, and keep the garments in dried rosemary. A leaf sticks to each of George's boots from the piles on the path side, reminding him that God is liberal, nature a spendthrift. 'Spend freely' is the message. 'Impendit'. Give cheerfully.

Heriot takes on two apprentices in his shop, or booth, and a servant, such is his confidence.

His neighbour, David Brown, notices the rise to fame, standing in George's booth of an evening, watching him work,

'Weel Heriot, I heard by trumpet at the Mercat Cross, ye're declarit goldsmith to the Queen, 'fir a' the dayis o' his life'. A job foriver, Heriot, ye've a job foriver,'

George does not look up, 'No foriver, Davy – a'll no live foriver.'

'Ye micht, ye micht. They as believe in Life Eternal.'

Davy crosses himself, then remembers himself, and looks behind to see no one is looking.

George laughs, 'A'll no be makin rings as gifts fur the Queen's ambassadors in heaven.'

Davy smiling says, 'Wha kens whit ye'll dae. Mebbe the saints have a likin fur rings.'

'Niver! But this I ken, a'm makin rings the nicht, twa o' them.'

'That'll bring in the siller, man.'

'And send it oot. I send it oot furst. Spend siller to earn siller.'

George is happy to work for his Queen only for promises of payment, promises recorded by the Chancellor. This gives Anna her head; she orders with glee, giving gifts to any visitor from abroad that brings good news.

'Your brother is well, your Grace,' says a voyager from Denmark and she bestows a costly jewel. When she can afford no more, or the Chancellor says no, she lends George an 'old' diamond pendant, or a brooch, or an emerald from last year, until the debt is paid, or until he makes it into something else. This year he has so many of her 'old' jewels that the King has to ask the chancellor to use tax money to buy them back. Anna may not know that emeralds are more precious than rubies, but Heriot knows that Anna is more precious than emeralds.

He is their pawnbroker and moneylender: it is a dangerous line to tread, he can still be afraid, he knows that two of his predecessors, in the trade of royal jewellers were hanged.

'My Queen shall be decoratit!' Bawls the King. 'Get her jewels oot o' pawn!' He is as angry now with his Chancellor as he was once with his Lord Bothwell. But now the King's confidence and expectation of wealth to come have grown with proof of his young Queen's fruitfulness: three children in six years, and Anna not yet twenty-five. That is real power and glory, especially when the Queen of England has no issue. He swiftly realises that his greatest asset is Anna his Queen and that she must be decorated as much as she desires, if not more.

Rosehips – bloated, overripe, but bright red as bloodstains still dot the pathways. Old Mrs Heriot gathers them for their medicinal value. She takes them to Mary the Heriots' maid and together they scrape away the seeds inside and use the thin red shells to boil and keep as a syrup in case of winter coughs.

'The Visitor' is the name given to the illness old Mrs Heriot dreads, visitor because on a young and healthy person it comes and goes. But to a child or old person it is a deathly visit. And so it comes to pass that The Visitor is at the Palace. One of the elderly advisors coughed himself into a fitful sleep from which he never woke. Now the infant Princess Margaret is making a noise like the bark of a dog with her little cough. The Queen is distressed. Old Mrs Heriot starts scraping and boiling rosehips and pushing her son to take the syrup up to the Palace. George refuses, as he knows that way trouble lies. If the medicine does not work, he can be accused of poisoning – and there are jealousies and enemies enough among Palace officials who will accuse.

'I'll tell them aboot it mither. Like as not the Queen's doctor has the same.'

The Queen's doctor does not believe in such old wives' tales. Science is his master. He knows that what the little Princess needs is cupping on her back which means little glass cups heated on a flame and stuck to the back till they draw the blood out through the skin into large blisters. The child is just over a year and still a baby, still needing milk to drink. She howls in pain as the blood is drawn from the back of her little chest and each time she catches a breath she barks painfully her panting cough which racks the whole tiny body.

'I watch and am as a sparrow alone upon the housetop.'

On the death of Princess Margaret, George hands back the copy of Psalm 102.

Eight

1600 – A fruitful vine
by the side of thine house

There is no stopping him now. James and Anna have a fourth child and second son, Charles. James gives praise to the good Lord God Almighty, whose obvious intention it is to increase the wealth and power of the House of Stuart by making him heir to the English throne. And all because of that fruitful wife, for whom jewels are a celebration of her success. He is not above boasting to his Lords and Counsellors.

'Keep at it, your Grace as ye niver ken how lang bairns will live,' advises Melville; but Huntly takes a different approach, ' Upricht love is rewardit by steidy growthe.'

Huntly's wife is the Queen's Gentlewoman and this is ill-liked because the Huntlys favour the old religion; they still practice as Catholics in secret. But James will not upset his

Queen – even when he can see she is not shaping up as a true Calvinist. Anna has a Lutheran priest and repeats when asked of it: 'by Grace alane, through Faith alane on the basis of Scripture alane'. She takes the Lutheran Eucharist. James tries to keep it secret, but there are no secrets in a Palace. The world quickly hears of every thought, intention and motive. James makes his intentions and motives clear, so that Queen Elizabeth's English advisors will know that he fully intends to keep to the Protestant faith and that all around him should also. His thoughts he keeps to himself. To keep his Queen happy and producing children is his route to a new kingdom.

Each day he repeats the Lord's Prayer, which Anna calls the Our Father.

"Thy kingdom come," takes on a new meaning, but he keeps that to himself also.

However, he is perplexed by the constant warnings of his advisors about his wife. They emphasize that the Queen of Scotland may have Catholic sympathies. A gaggle of Huntly, Maitland, Lennox, Bathgate, Clifford and who else he cannot remember stand around with heat in their voices.

'No just sympathies, Highness. She partakes o' the faith. She has receivit Communion in the infidel religion spawned o' the Great Whore at least nine times.'

'Stop it Maitland. You do your cause nae good by this Great Whore rubbish.'

'The cheek is enough, he canna speak o' the Queen and the Great Whore in the same breath.' James stands up.

Maitland, trying to correct himself, replies, 'Forgie me your Grace but I was not speaking o' Queen Anna here but o' Queen Mary your mother.'

James steps forward, barely containing his anger.

'Banish him.'

'A figure of speech. Dinna repeat it. But beware uprisin's, beware witches, beware rebellions. A' spawned from the same beast begat by the Great Whore.'

Lennox sides with Maitland,

'Nine times she has taken Catholic Communion. Nine times it has been spied on since the departure of her own Lutheran priest for the true faith',

'Her priest became a Presbyterian Minister, your Highness. He convertit to the one true Scottish Kirk.'

'But he is a Dane.'

'He doesna have tae convert. A Lutheran is protesting. No' like a Calvinist ye unnerstan, and closer to the Catholics. But nanetheless, a Protester.'

Huntly stands forward. 'May I advise your Grace that there was a clause in your marriage Treaty, whereby you receivit 150,000 pounds Scots which securit the Queen's right to Lutheran worship.'

'Aye, that freedom is paid for, sire.'

'Now she doesnae have her own priest, no' even a Lutheran. So whar will she gang if oor ain Scots cleric is coorse and ill-mainert?'

'She maun convert to the true faith, just as her own Danish Lutheran convertit.'

'Willintly?'

Lennox clenches his fist and makes a grimace, 'Wha wouldna do it willintly knawin that the fires o' Hell await those wha dinna?'

James is not impressed by Lennox's histrionics.

'It's that Lady Jane Drummond, sire,' interrupts Bathgate.

'Her Gentlewoman?' replies the King. 'She is fair and guid and the Queen loves her.'

'Her brother's a poet, so she maun be a Catholic.'

Thoughtfully, Clifford joins in at last, 'That is not enough reason. Elizabeth Melville is the finest poet o' oor time and she is a great Calvinist and will be kent as the first and grandest lady makar and defender o' the Faith.'

'I am scunnert, my Lords,' says James. 'You mak bletherskite. To hunting, my Lord Huntly, ma bonny brither on steed. Bring the dugs. Awa' ye go.'

'And the question o' Lady Drummond?'

'Bring her poet brither tae court and let's see if he's a Pape.'

And with that James and Huntly sweep out of the Hall. Lennox walks to the end of the Palace and asks to be admitted to the Queen. She and Lady Drummond are in the Queen's Audience chamber, the room with the carved arms of the King's grandmother on the ceiling – Mary de Guise-Lorraine, a fleur de lys and double cross, the links with the great Catholic monarchies of southern Europe. The cabinet behind the Queen, black and silver with large, central red tortoiseshell hearts, is known to have belonged to the King's mother, and no one took it out when she was executed. Not the King certainly. The red hearts in tortoiseshell shine, pulsating, he imagines, with dangerous life as Lennox is shown in, his anger gone.

Shy now, he asks, 'His Grace wishes tae invite my Lady Drummond's brither, William o' Hawthornden for a hearing.'

Jane Drummond curtseys to the Earl, 'I shall see tae it.' And Lennox leaves.

Once the door has closed, Jane turns to her Queen and asks,

'An honour or an inquisition?'

'An honour, it maun onlie be seen as an honour. He will bring his sonnets and madrigals.'

'I ken they question my faith,' says Lady Drummond.

'But there isnae proof,' replies the Queen. 'There is niver proof unless you wish to be saintit.'

Lady Drummond adds, 'There maun be a freedom in faith.'

To which Queen Anna replies, 'When I was a child I was invitit tae my cousin Mecklenbourg in the sooth o' Denmark for a stay o' twa months. Wi' her I went tae daily Mass in their chapel celebratit bi a priest wha laughed and smiled and always ate wi us. A couthier man I niver met before, so blythe and full o' happiness, naething like a 'man o' God'.

Here she imitates a disapproving Lennox, mimicking him, 'There'll be nae laughing on the Sabbath Day!' She continues, 'But there in Denmark I remember the hale hoosehold was infused wi' his joyfu' spirit. He gave thanks, and it really was thanks, no' obsequy, tae God afore each meal and always wi'oot fear.'

'Our faith needna be full o' fear,' explains Jane, 'so then why is it? Why am I feart for William to be examined on his faith, if it be a happy faith, far fae Lennox and his hell fires?'

'He willna be examined. He will be invitit for Oor entertainment to sing sonnets and madrigals, of which I ken from you he has some. That will satisfy the demand. There is to be no mention of religion, but all merriment.'

'My brother is sixteen years old, your Grace, a student of Latin, Aristotole, humanities and theology at the University here in Edinburgh.'

'All the better. One sonnet and one madrigal.'

'He will be honourt to please your Graces. But let there be no talk o' the Great Whore, he willna understaun the meaning.'

'Lennox canna keep whores oot o' his mind, but there may be muckit reasons for that,' suggests Lady Huntly who has been listening silently sewing a border.

The evening of entertainment for young William Drummond's visit brings more Lords than expected, linked as it is to the gossip of the Queen's religion. Some think that a public questioning is in order, but the Queen has requested madrigals and sonnets and dancing, and other musicians and poets, so that William is lost in the throng of talent set before the Court. It is known that James falls asleep to the Queen's entertainments, and Jane Drummond has advised her brother of this. William Drummond has therefore composed a perfect short madrigal on the subject of the King's favourite passion; and as he stands before the assembled lords and ladies in their finery, the first notes of the lute sound, the court is silent. A single string is plucked and the fine voice of youth sings clearly:

'This world a Hunting is,
The Prey poore Man, The Nimrod fierce is Death,
His speedie Grei-hounds are,
Lust, sicknesse, Envie, Care,
Strife that neere falls amisse,
With all those ills which haunt us while wee breath.
Now, if (by chance) wee flie,
Of these the eager Chase,
Old Age with stealing Pace,
Castes up his Nets, and there wee panting die.'

As the last notes of the lute fall silent, the audience remain also silent for some time. A hush on the merry crowd, a philosophical silence. And the King, given both to hunting and equally to a melancholic turn of thought, bursts into applause. Lennox jostles close as the crowd erupts into clapping, following the King in his approval and whispers in the royal ear, 'Chatecheeze him now. Ask if he's a Papist.'

Angrily the King replies,

'Hark to the boy, Lennox! It matters not our releegion. We will a' die anyway, if not by hunting then of old age.'

Nine

'The highest bench
is the sliddriest to sit upon'

So James wrote in his book of advice to his young son, which he calls Basilikon Doron. It is a manual of wisdom on how a king should rule his people. The sliddriest question of all at this time is the punishing of Catholics. James' greatest friend and liveliest companion, most inspired trencher-mate and debater of things godly is supposed by many to be a Catholic. The Earl of Huntly from Strathbogie Castle in Aberdeenshire is light of heart. He laughs more easily and argues more passionately, and Maitland wants him dead.

James protests; churches, crosses and shrines have been smashed by the Great Reform and is this necessary? Now the happy people too must be annihilated – and to what end? Huntly implies when deeply questioned that God's creation is good, that nature is good, that art is good and mankind himself at the base, good. He cannot imagine that anyone would do him harm.

'Huntly is a fool,' says Maitland who is a canny organizer and hard worker and planner. Maitland believes that the world is but a snare, all creation a tangle of temptations for the pilgrim soul, and when pressed says, the Catholic Church is 'the mither o' harlots, auld in adulteries, the mistress o' witchcrafts. She will shaw the nations her bare-skud, and the kingdoms her shame, who shall lastly hate the hure, mak her desolate, eat her flesh and burn her wi' fire.'

Maitland says this with his voice rising as the King becomes more and more desirous of the company of his merry Huntly.

Maitland calls him 'Huntly the Harlot' and has no doubt that he is a bugger.

On a seat less slippery sits George Heriot, pleased to remain what he considers a worker, an artisan, a 'makar' of fine jewels and plate, not a man concerned with matters of politics or religion. He notices the first cracks in the fallen leaves covered by frost and as the first chilled winds of winter blow, the leaves are chasing each other like golden birds up the paths to the Palace. He is here again to consult on a jewel for her Grace.

'Tae stert I propone golden birds, thinly beat, linkit yin tae thither alang a chain o' pearls, or mebbe no' the pearls, mebbe better just plain birds alane.'

Anna protests, 'Plain? No' you for unsonsie too. There is too much blether o' plainness. Let's have some diamonds and rubies stuck inside...'

George catches the drift, 'The birdies eyes sapphires, and in the beaks a gem, each bird tae inbring a gem wi' its beak.'

Anna claps her hands, 'Oh, you have sic guid ideas, George. I shall order a lang chain o' these birds.'

The Queen tells the King and the King tells the Chancellor and the Chancellor says, 'Naw.'

There is money for a chain of Crosses full of gems, but not for 'any other sign or signal of idolatrie.'

The Queen does not want a chain of crosses, she has enough crosses, but no birds at all, never has she been given a bird design.

'My Annie,' says the King, 'You are my sweet bedfellow, is that no enough?'

'No,' says Anna.

'Think o' our finances.' James is reading a letter from his cousin Queen Elizabeth which makes him smile, he reads it aloud, 'Remember that a bird of the air, if no other instrument, to an honest king shall stand instead of many feigned practices, to utter aught may anywise touch him.' A riddle, nae doot, but ye shall have your birdies, my Anna, my Queen, the letter brings guid fortune, another twa thoosand English pounds a year.'

A half-moon rises above the jagged trees as the smell of onions rises above the stairs in Fishmarket Close. A messenger arrives to say that Queen Anna calls her jeweller George Heriot again to the Palace. She commissions the chain of jewelled birds by borrowing the money from her jeweller himself. It is decided that evening with statement from Anna:

'Like geese, that flee fae Scotland, my birds will flee across my briest.'

George walks home to a clearer moon and starts work in his workshop at once.

He and Christian have a child now, a boy named after his father who is two years old. 'Wee Geordie,' they call him, though he is a large, strong and healthy child. Christian spends every hour of her waking day making sure he has proper food, clothing and protection from the illnesses and vapours that haunt the close streets of Edinburgh.

Rosehip syrup, from her mother-in-law, is a daily dosage as is milk and porridge, cheese and eggs. Wee Geordie grabs at meat from his mother's plate, but she does not let him have it yet. Christian is expecting another child and feels sleepy by seven o'clock when Geordie goes to bed. George is deprived of his wife's company on many evenings because of this, but his increased work means he sits at table with his ledger, rather than a companion, and his accounts are adding up well. He has decided to borrow money based on the value of the jewels he keeps in stock: as everyone knows he is the King's jeweller and he is for life, his position is clear and unshakeable. This money he then lends to the King and takes a percentage of interest. As he is only paying himself for jewels commissioned by Anna in the end, it is an amusing circuitous route for money to augment as it moves around his account ledger. It is only his ability to imagine and move these numbers on his page before him that increases his wealth. Christian would never understand it, though she is numerate, so it's good that she retires early to bed.

Lord Douglas wants buttons like the King's, in amethyst and gold, for his hunting waistcoat, and for the jacket on top. George asks for payment in advance for all works, no matter how long they take, then he lends this money to the King and Queen. So long as the courtiers are competitive, it's a merry round of making jewels, creating a fashion for the desperate to follow, taking jewels as surety and demanding payment in advance.

His neighbour, the corn operator, David Brown, calls in most nights.

'Are ye well, ye auld Jew,' is Brown's habitual greeting. George takes that as a compliment – Jews sell him gems, travelling from far across the earth with a glint in the eye and a warm smile, and tales from the East. He hears about camels and elephants, hot suns and miles of sand and weary journeys beneath the stars beyond places like Bethlehem, Jerusalem, Assyria and Greece. He works until daylight pours across the round oak table, picking out the crumbs and dust on top and brightening his open ledger, his quill and sand box. These are expensive acquisitions; a bound and sewn ledger is the mark of a man of means, especially if he has to fill it up himself.

Outside the leaves are piling beneath his feet on the dry mud, piling over his shoes in brown and yellow pieces, like little fish with no smell; the wind blows away the smell. He can't say that about Fishmarket Close, and his wife complains. Walking on the crags above the town he can see each house below; why build a town where everyone is overlooked? No wonder the King favours Stirling Castle, or Falkland or Linlithgow Palace.

Ten

1603 – Long live the King

But soon none of these Scots palaces are needed. On March 26th 1603, lathered horse and sweaty nobleman bring news of the death of Queen Elizabeth of England. Lord Carey jumps high off his steed in the forecourt of the Palace and is admitted entry at once, recognised by his livery and his face and his relationship with Lord Cecil. James has already been proclaimed King of England on the streets of London.

'The Queen is dead, long live King James the First.'

'James the First was yin o' my ancestors,' James reminds his messenger, who knows nothing of Scotland. None of them know anything about Scotland he will discover. Nonetheless, delighted, he cannot disguise his delight, though he must also show sorrow at the passing of his cousin.

At St Giles Church on the Royal Mile, James VI of Scotland and I of England, Wales and Ireland with his Queen Anna beside him, gives a harangue – an address to his people: 'I will retour here every three years.' Few believe him. Not with all that land and people to govern, the heavy hand of fate and the heavy dues of state, not to mention the great wealth and weight of office; the crown itself weighs more than a bag of gold.

'He's aff fur a guid job in London. He'll no' come back.'

'Oor Jamie. The English have bocht wir King. Ilka man is for sale.'

'At the right price'.

Soon they realize that even if the King rides south with all great speed, the Queen does not.

'She'll stay wi' the bairns.'

Her children are at Stirling Castle and at Linlithgow Palace. She gathers her loyal men, the Catholic lords, and a host of horsemen and rides at once to Stirling to see the boy she has been denied all these years. It is a bursting of a vein of desire held so long in check. Galloping along the lanes heavy with early blossom, Anna is told to slow down; she is pregnant again, for the sixth time. She slows to a walk breathing heavily under the blue skies, with the sunlight on her dress and the fur on her hood showing white around her head. She is smiling widely and triumphant. No one can stop her seeing her son Henry now.

The Earl and Countess of Mar cannot forbid the tired and panting queen to ride up the high streets that lead to the great castle gates and the spiral cobbled route to the door itself and she is followed by dozens of men. A groom rushes to hold her horse and help her alight, another steps forward to support her,

'Welcome your Grace, your chaumer is ready.'

And my Prince?

The Prince will not be brought, on the King's orders he is not to leave unless with the King's express permission.

Anna collapses in a bed and waits. She eats, sleeps and refuses to leave until her son leaves with her. Enough days pass for a letter from the King. Lord Fyvie arrives from Edinburgh. He is going to deliver the news to the Queen that she must travel to London and leave all the children in Scotland to be brought up by their wards.

Fyvie enters her chamber and she knows what he is about to say,

'Nooooooo!'

The high-pitched scream resounds for the castle to hear. Anna has had enough of bearing children that she cannot see. Here at Stirling, where she bore her first son Henry, she will now destroy the sixth. Before Fyvie has time to open his mouth, she is beating her pregnant belly with a force that knows no reason.

'I will niver leave Henry again.' She sobs, 'I dinna care if I die. Do what you will wi' me now.'

She howls and collapses on the floor; her women come and pick her up, bleeding, from the floor. They lead her to a chamber where she miscarries a baby boy.

***

A wren gives a reedy call on the branch of an apple tree. It hops and chirps forward boldly in George's direction, a chaffinch appears and a blackbird and George knows finally that spring has arrived and with it news of change. Huge change is upon him and all his house. The Queen announces she will stay in Scotland. She will not be separated from her children. It is bad enough with her in Edinburgh and them all a day's ride away, but in London she will never even hear their news. Her winning card is to refuse to join her King. There are enough nobles in Scotland to support her desires for a Catholic rule. Now that James has left with all his disapproving Protestant advisors, those left behind are of a mind not to be ruled from England. When the court leaves, then the wealth leaves, the excitement and gossip, the commissions and songs. The Queen can become a regent for Prince Henry and secure for him a match with a Catholic house in Europe – a Spanish princess to secure an Alliance against England.

However Henry is not such a malleable child. He loves his father and reads his father's printed letter in the form of Basilikon Doron, advice to a prince, and now widely distributed all over London. The English perceive what a wise and scholarly King they now have and what is more important, a fertile one, with three live children and another expected. News soon reaches the King that the expected is no longer expected, and that it was a male child.

'If the Queen is bent on such destruction of her own body and family, then what is she capable of doing to the country?'

'Give in to all her desires, let her see Henry and travel with all the children to London.'

'But a wicked Papist upstart queen should be put to the sword. A raging whore of Babylon.'

Lennox has again to be stopped and shut up – Maitland puts his hand over his mouth.

'What he means Majesty is that he will see to it at once, letters will be sent and escort arranged and the royal family will travel together.'

George and Christian Heriot hope they don't have to leave Edinburgh, their home and family and life and the High Street. They are part of the Queen's retinue and followers. George is the Queen's Jeweller for Life, and Queen Anna relies on George for much more than jewels: advice, money, good sense. They will go where the Queen goes and hope she stays in Scotland. When George hears of the news of her lost baby, he is more than worried. She cannot be in her right mind and must stay at least till she is better.

George is not a noble and will not get a place in the company that surrounds the Queen; he will have to make his own way south. Christian with her two little boys does not relish a journey by horse to London with danger of thieves and brigands. George says he will send them safely and gently by ship from Leith, while he rides to London on Pricker, the horse he has now after all been persuaded to buy.

'We'll cowp a house in London wi' more daylight.' He tries to reassure Christian. 'And there will be no smell o' fish guts a' day.'

Christian smiles. 'We'll be brave.' But she is afraid. She has never been outside of Edinburgh before – even Leith is a mystery.

In the last gleam of daylight, a dead oak claws the sky. Christian looks at the orange and grey fingers of clouds behind the toothless giant of a ruin on the hill. 'Aiblins England will be greener and pleasanter.'

'And warmer.'

She holds wee Geordie's hand. He looks trustingly up at her face, and sucks his fat fingers, his face shiny with spit. Johnny lies in her arms, a sleeping bundle of five months; he smells purely of milk and bairn, which to Christian is the nearest thing to the smell of Heaven.

***

God's appointed King makes his way south more confidently than his jeweller's wife.

He takes a full month, conferring knighthoods as he goes, a triumphant trail through the noble houses of England, each vying for favour; he is so thrilled with his new thrones and flattered by the attention of families who live far more splendidly than he as King of Scotland has ever done himself. These noble families are quite aware of the Scots King's apparent poverty, but they refrain from passing unkind comments.

Cleverest of all is Robert Cecil of Theobalds, whose house is the calculated triumph of its owner. There is fellow feeling between this short and bent man, like a dwarf, and the King, no perfect specimen himself. Theobalds has more great art and luxury than James has ever seen; with its courtyards, fountains, elaborate gardens. There are turrets of rosy bricks and a loggia with walls painted with the history of England, to which James is being added. A green hall lined with artificial trees, complete with bark and birds' nests – and hunting grounds as far as the eye can see.

The King loves being outside above all. He rides better than he can dance, or even walk, his foot is turned outwards too much, but on horseback he borrows the elegance of his steed.

He is wakened with a welcome call, 'The sun shines, the dogs are ready, the air is meet for hunting.'

'Every boar that ever there was will gather here, for certain, because today's the day our Great King goes a-hunting.' Sings a handsome new courtier.

'Deer, partridge, heron.'

The youth lists the game that abound in Theobalds' forests while he hands over some splendid clothing which appears to be already made to fit King James.

Trees lose their limbs all the time and while hunting there in the soft woodlands following deer trails at Theobalds, a branch falls on him and the King's arm snaps like a twig as a tree catches him and leaves his own limb dangling by his side. Cecil has the best doctor in the land come to set it. His stay with Cecil lasts longer, some say extended on purpose by the cunning nobleman. But there is plague in London, and their move must be delayed. When he finally arrives at the Palace in London, his arm is in a white sling.

Eleven

Sea voyage

Christian Heriot boards the ship at Leith in May 1603. Towering above her like a floating castle, the hull has little windows in the wood – composed of trees in their hundreds. The day is wet and the planks are slippery on the walk up the gangway. She carries the baby in one arm while with the other holds carefully onto the rope bannister. Behind her walks wee Geordie with the wet-nurse and Mary their maid, both having to leave their families for what they certainly see as forever, watching their parents weeping silently on the quayside. They do not know when the ship will sail. They must wait for a wind but there is no wind in the heavy drizzle. Passengers are meant to board last, but men with barrels and livestock still keep climbing up like ants with crumbs. So much food is needed for such a short voyage.

Men who on shore are disordered drunkards change once on ship, each knowing their task and sticking to it with speed. All foodstuffs in the focsle tied down, coils of ropes neatly at hand, sails folded, and a captain on the poop deck.

'Poop deck, poop deck, poop deck,' repeats wee Geordie as he skips along ahead of Mary, laughing and looking fearlessly into the eyes of the sailors, who wink and encourage him.

One informs the boy and Mary that actual poops are delivered over the side of the ship. He shows them the sailors' privy. Christian calls her son and maid back at once to catch up and see their cabin, which is no more than a cupboard with shelves for sleeping.

'You are in the luxury quarters as befits a wife o' the Court,' comments the sailor of rank that George has charged with their welfare. He is not joking; the cabin is on the highest deck and near to the Captain's.

That evening with the moon just past its full and the wind in the right direction, the *Thin Lizzie* sets sail. Though named after the late and probably slim Queen Beth, her figurehead is a huge wooden woman with yellow hair loose and breasts akimbo. She is crudely carved, and this rude depiction of womanhood disturbs Christian even after she has entered the absurdly small cabin and is overseeing the midwife feed Johnny. The child sleeps on the narrow bed, while the ladies stand outside and watch the moonrise over the sea.

And there, more brilliant and splendid than any court jewel cut even for a King, hangs the moon. Reflected in the water like another limpid pearl, it lights the small horizontal clouds with silver under navy, as Christian is called in to dinner by the Captain. She leaves her companions, who aim to get wee Geordie to sleep before going below deck to eat.

'And mynd tae lock the cabin,' she calls.

'Fat, salt mutton wi' venison collops,' announces the cook.

It sticks in Christian's throat as wine is poured.

'A fine nicht for sailing?' asks one Lord who is moving with the herd to London but wants a smoother passage and to bring his extensive wardrobe under his own guard. He, Leslie, is happy that the Kings Jeweller's wife is there to win favour with and further decorate his clothing, which he feels, is sure to impress the English court. He wears fine cork heels on his shoes, extending his height – a gamble on board ship even in a small wind.

'The smaw the wind, the mair sleekit the bracky-bree, the harder the wind the faster we go but shooglie underfoot.' The Captain glances at Leslie's shoes.

'For those who wish to be sick there are buckets in the luxury cabins,' calls an English man.

Christian had noticed the stained wooden receptacle in her cabin. She cannot eat the meat but sips the wine and dips her bread in it, watching the red soak into the white.

'Don't be feart, Mistress Heriot,' Interrupts Leslie, 'Efter the first nicht, you get used to life abuird ship. It wilna be lang till we reach London.'

'How lang?' she asks.

'That depends on the guid winds and the Guid Lord,' answers the Captain, 'We howp in less than a month,' and when Christian gasps, 'I ayways says less than a month as that wis the langest it iver took.'

'And my Lord Carey took twa days and a half to ride tae Edinburgh to give the King notice of the guid Queen's death.'

'Aye but how many horses?'

'They changit every three hours, and he didna sleep.'

'All to gain that post he now has as Gentleman o' the Bedchamber, closest to the king, but the King will need an Englishman to advise on the English ways, the fashions and the manners at court.'

'The King will bring his own fashions and manners,' replies Leslie, determined to leave a sartorial mark.

The smell of the cold, salty, fat mutton and the churning of the boat along with the heady wine make Christian dizzy. 'I maun leave.' She whispers.

Leslie rises at once and escorts her to her cupboard cabin where the two servants are already snoring and the smell of Geordie's poop fills the air. Christian collapses on her narrow bed. Lying there she can feel the wooden boards on either side encasing her and sensing safety from the rolling and tipping ship, she falls asleep, thinking she will change clothing in the morning.

But morning brings a greater swell upon the ocean further out into the North Sea where the wind and salt spray hit her face with a force as she seeks the privy. She is suddenly tipped to the side and hangs for her life onto the railing. A sailor catches her and drags her back to the cabin.

'Stay inside. Use the bucket.'

The bucket has been used twice by the maids and once by Geordie, who is now up and jumping to look out the window.

'Mammy I spy the sea!' he yells, 'Mammy I spy the sea.'

Christian can only lie between the boards of her bed for safety, to avoid the lurching floor and her lurching stomach. She cannot get to the bucket in time and vomits onto the floor where the boards are far apart and liquid falls through to the deck below. A yell comes from below, but Christian passes out.

Time passes, as it always does, without anyone managing to stop it. Waves crash, the ship tilts too far, water is let in on board, and slooshes off the poop deck, dripping inside. Ships biscuits and water are thrown into the cabin and the women are told to stay still.

The baby sleeps, stuck onto the nipples of the wet-nurse but Geordie yells and shouts.

Suddenly the room is full of water. The door is open. It happens fast. The ship is on one side, only to tip to the other and baby, Geordie and wet-nurse slip outside onto the deck. Mary chases after, grabbing Geordie, but she falls over too and they all disappear like bundles of laundry in the white raging foam.

Christian is saved by being wedged in the narrow bunk and does not even know what is going on. She might as well be dead.

As the ship nears the Thames, Lord Leslie thinks she is dead. He prepares a letter for Heriot, and goes to the cabin to see to the corpse. Lying in the wooden cupboard with her face to the boards, Christian Heriot is pale and grey as the sky. Leslie bends and takes the left hand, where her ring finger carries a small, expertly wrought emerald ring, and he tries to loosen it.

Christian wakes indignantly and sits up. It is then that she feels the sudden dead weight of herself. Her eyes widen and now she can see from the expression on his face and the letter in his hand that the worst has happened. She does not need to be told, but Leslie confirms that her maids and children are gone. She slumps back on the coffin like wooden boards.

'There is no point,' she tells Leslie. 'Write saying I am dead.'

Twelve

The Word of the Lord

There are few courtiers in London since George arrived, on account of the Plague. The King and Queen after a speedy coronation have left the city with as many as possible; any court official who has a country house is gone. George does not. In this he counts his lucky stars, for there are some that he can see – less competition for a good lodging. He has found a house, in the parish of St Martin in the Fields, not far from the Palace of Westminster, the Palace of St James and the Palace of Whitehall. He is near to the city for the jewel trade, near to the river for transport but with a sunlit house and pleasant garden of his own.

He is waiting on the Thames for the *Thin Lizzie* to dock and let down her boats. Word reaches him by mouth along the quayside of the disaster and the loss of his two sons and maids. Stunned, he holds himself.

'Are ye siccar? Is that true?' He can't believe it. But Christian is alive, in that he can rejoice. He must hold himself for her.

Heavy with sorrow, Christian is escorted by Leslie off the ship onto a boat and rowed over to George. Leslie is without shoes and looks more shocked than Christian; his precious wardrobe, his entire clothing has been washed overboard.

The jeweller embraces his wife, who finally sobs in his arms.

'Take a kerchief, there is plague about,' suggests a new servant – a mature and sensible looking woman called Rachel. A closed carriage brings the family to their new home.

Christian, like a creature risen from the dead, pushes the heavy, studded oak door, which creaks over the dry flags. Leaves have blown in and the crack of crushing one under her foot startles her. A large, polished oak table, circular with space for twelve persons stands in the hall. Three windows, arched with diamond shaped leaded panes of glass light the hall from high above her. A wolf hound with longing eyes sidles up to her.

'He came wi' the house, though I willna hunt.'

'You can learn.'

'No. None of that wastery. I like to wark. For you, Christian and our future bairns.'

'Children' corrects Ruth.

'Children, for our children I will wark.'

Christian loses her energy at the mere thought and sinks onto a bench, tears falling again from her eyes.

***

At St James' Palace, Anna is smiling, dressed in heavy, ornate clothing that she is obviously unaccustomed to wearing and trying out for the first time. She can hardly believe what she sees before her.

'And mair jewels Heriot.'

A huge casket, carried by matching pageboys in full gold edged livery, enters, brimming with the jewellery once belonging to Queen Elizabeth.

'The auld maids of the late Queen delivered these to me at the border. But the jewels are too like the withered maids, no' bright and gey enough. They want new settings and mair style. George, ye can new-fangle them for oor younger court.'

Overwhelmed, George's eyes widen.

Ever resourceful, he bows,

'As your Majesty biddins.' Wondering if the strong young pages come with the heavy casket, whether there is a guard, where he must take them and, praying for inspiration, he promises, 'I shall tak ten each day,' knowing he can only reasonably work one in a day, 'returning the next e'en with your favourite.' That would have to be the one.

'Ye ken whit I favour, George,' replies Anna.

King James enters, comes near and touches his sleeve.

'I am thankful for a Scots jeweller, a jeweller for all my days.'

Lord Cecil is never far behind James, advising on the necessities and the calendar.

'You know we need a flash of gems for the official entry to London before the people. The plague is nearly over and there is demand for your presence. You will process in some triumph before your loyal English subjects, who expect a royal show.'

'Ye can depend on me, my Lord,' replies George.

'Must we flaunt ourselves before the mass of people?' asks James.

Cecil advises, 'The late Queen, God rest her soul, did love to show herself.'

James, quickly, 'Show? God's wounds, I shall pull down my britches and they shall see my hurdies.'

Cecil delivers a tight smile.

Anna, not listening to her husband, pulls out a string of black pearls, at least three feet long,

'Now this loup is too short... George...'

James paces. 'I am of a mind that I maun thank God for this bounty, our great guid fortuin, not only these our jewels which are but proof o' His almighty wit and benificence, but these we faw heir til, that we may rule in peace and quateness: four nations agin oor common foes. We werena given this wealth for no reason.'

Anna looks at him, and James continues,

'My dear heart, you maun be pleasit and we have appointit for life, just like your faither the Danish King, a court playwright – and his troop to be ca'ed henceforth The Kings Men. His masques will be halesome and edifying for our courtiers and guests. But God has called me for a grander purpose, to unite all in a single translation of His Word.'

Anna is not listening to the bit about translation; she has become fascinated by a large diamond.

James calls for a more responsive audience. 'My Lord Northampton, Mr Buchanan! Bring them to me.'

James is in a state of high excitement. 'Quickly'.

'My Lords, let it be known that there shall be a great thanksgiving to God, in the form of my ain metrical translation of the psalms which was begun when I was a bairn.'

For this they need call the Bishops, Lords and leading Puritans, who expand the plan. Soon it is not just the Psalms, and not just by James, in fact not even by James. He cannot be expected with the affairs of state to burden himself with mere translations; leave that to the experts.

At the first meeting James hears the first question from Dr Buchanan, his old friend,

'Are you for the Presbytery, and the strict Genevan discipline, or are you for Bishops and ceremonies, your Majestie?'

'Both,' answers the King with energy, 'I am for it all.'

'Good,' says an elder Lord. 'Then we must have a satisfying division of labour.'

The Bishop of Oxford speaks up; he has it all worked out already: 'Let there be fifty-four translators, divided into six committees, two in Oxford, two in Cambridge and two in Westminster.'

'So I can keep an eye on them,' puts in James.

'Let the tone be simple and avoid complex phrasing,' offers a Puritan.

'When the word has multiple meanings,' says the Bishop in coloured robes, 'we should follow the early church fathers where possible. For example the Greek 'ecclesia' is to be 'church', not 'congregation' as preferred by the Puritans.'

'A Puritan is a Protestant frayed out of his wits,' says James, and he continues, to their great embarrassment. 'How they used that puir lady my mither is not unkent. And wi grief I may remember it: she did desire, only, a private chapel, wherein to serve God, efter her airt, wi' some few select bodies; but her Supremacy was not suffeecient to procur it at their hauns.' He felt the pain as a child. 'How they dealt with me in my minoritee, you all kent; it wisna done saicretfu, and, though I'd fain conceal it, I canna. I will expoond it thus.' He puts his hand on the jewel in his hat, he speaks to the lords and bishops. 'If the bishops were oot o' pouer,' James claims, 'and the Puritans in place, I ken what wid become o' my Supremacy'.

'We all know the Puritans will not give up the argument lightly,' advises the wise bishop.

'I will mak them conform, or I will harry them oot o' the land,' retorts James.

'No,' replies his Bishop, 'you will just keep them infernally busy, overseeing translations from Hebrew, Greek and Latin. This great work will take many years.'

'Where does power at Court end? With Bishops or the King?'

'Look on the chess board, my lord. The King is supreme, but he is stuck. He cannot move like a Bishop.'

'But when the King is lost, the game is lost.'

'So we guard thee well.'

Lord Pembroke, a Herbert, twenty-three years of age and handsome as a devil, enters and goes straight up to the King, who kisses him on the cheek.

Pembroke says, 'I thank you for my pardon and for the frog that you did put down my neck.'

'You deservit a puddock doon the neck, but that is all, not banishing or jailing, for all you did was get a maid o' honour boukit.'

'Yes, but it was the late Queen's maid, and so went her honour.'

The King laughs.

'When you are merrit, you are rewardit for sic hochhurhudie. We shall find ye a good maid. And was that also your jest, young Pembroke? A piglet in my stool-closet?'

'Bring on the piglet.'

A page in bright, green, gold-edged livery enters carrying a struggling piglet, which is wearing a matching hat.

There is general laughter as the King asks, 'Do you recognize this fellow?' Pembroke takes the piglet in his arms. Courtiers try to keep laughing, but the King looks solemn for a moment and remembers a line from his Psalms.

'As a jewel in a pig's snout, so is a fair woman without discretion.'

That is what Buchanan would say, but where is Buchanan? I have a project for him.'

Thirteen

Beggarly Scots and hopeful seed

By candlelight in a corner of the King's audience room, long before James makes an entry, some noblemen wait and the Fool is playing with sock puppets:

Left puppet: 'When can we rid ourselves of the blue-bonneted beggars in the King's Bedchamber?'

Right puppet: 'Bedchamber bulging with blue-bonneted beggars and bold buggers.'

Left puppet: 'I know a woman poisoner, she makes gowns for court.'

Right puppet: 'If ye canna kill them off, at least prevent them breeding. Poison is an easy one, especially for wives and babies.'

The new Earl of Southampton interrupts, 'Do you value your life, young Fool?'

Left puppet: 'The young always think they are immortal.'

Right puppet: 'Never a thought of death.'

Lord Southampton interrupts the puppets: 'It's a painful death for a poisoner, worse than a Papist.'

But the Left puppet replies: 'Worse than a treacherous Pape?'

Lord Southampton prompts: 'Hung, drawn and quartered, or crushed under a stone, you can choose.'

Northampton says loudly, 'We love the Gentlemen of the Bedchamber, I just wish I could understand them. Why can't they speak the Queen's English?

Essex chips in, 'Because they speak the King's Scots.'

The Fool jumps up, 'I wish I'd said that.'

'Say all ye want, young Fool, it willna change a jot.' James speaks. He is listening behind the blue trees, red hats and baying hounds of a hunting tapestry. He lifts the heavy fold and strides out with the Scots Gentlemen of the Bedchamber who have blue hats and red hose.

The Scots Kerr, recently made Lord Buckingham, draws his sword.

'Pit past, Kerr, you're anither bawheid,' James says. 'My Lords, if ye canna understaud oor tongue, then study more diligently. Translation is a felicity 'ut ita dicam', as Abelard says to Eloise.'

He pivots on his foot.

'I thocht we were here to plan the hunt.'

'No, your Majestie, the translation.'

'Aha', he is at once excited.

Puritans and Bishops crowd into the room again, in a feast of black woollen cloth on the left of the Hall and a glitter of bright robes on the right.

The King glistens in the middle wearing huge diamonds, emeralds and rubies, the symbols of majesty far transcending the jewels available to ordinary mortals. And here he will assert again his knowledge of Scripture, his knowledge of languages and above all his Divine right as King of Scotland, England, Ireland and Wales.

'Let us no' forget France,' announces Buckingham. 'The King's mither was Queen o' France, and therefore has a right to that throne forby.'

No wonder James loves the young Buckingham so much, he brings James' mother once more into the family fold, at the very court and before the very nobles who beheaded her. Life has come full circle.

'This Bible will be dedicated to James, King of Great Britain, France and Ireland.'

'By the Grace of God, King of Great Britain, France and Ireland.'

'Only by God's Grace of course,' James admits, 'and put "Defender of the Faith" after that.'

'And Prince Henry, what about the Prince?'

'Add "and to his hopeful seed". We cannot tempt fate.'

'Your hopeful seed, your Majesty, your glorious hopeful seed.'

'Only because of my seed am I here, and for such I thank my good Queen Anna.'

'Queen Anne, your Majesty, Anne in England.'

And here as if on cue, Anne, resplendent in gem-stiffened gown with hair bedecked and arrayed like a goddess, enters and all gasp. The effect is well expected. It has taken three full hours and ten ladies to dress her – thirty working hours immediately but hundreds before if the workmanship of the dress is counted; a pleated and jewelled art-work in itself, and the ruff, a fine gossamer lace, starched to stand around her graceful neck. Single drops of giant pearls hang from her ears, and a double string around her neck and across her body. She is thirty-one and in her prime, beautiful, and pregnant for the seventh time.

Here all her wishes are being fulfilled. Freed from any involvement in politics by the eager young bucks at court, she commissions plays and masques. James governs the Bible and its translation and she is responsible for Shakespeare's job for life, his promotion to The Kings Men. She procures stabililty for her favoured Makars: George Heriot and William Shakespeare. Both enter with her, as do Inigo Jones and Ben Jonson. The hall is becoming crowded with the King's company of bickering Puritans and Bishops and the Queen's artists.

The Queen's entry gently reminds him that business is over for the day.

'We shall see Love's Labour Lost,' says the Queen.

'I hope not,' replies the King and continues, more seriously, but unconsciously fingering his codpiece, 'My hopeful seeds are love's labour.'

'You are drole, dear Majesty, but Love's Labour Lost is the title of the play for this evening. Your company is here, the Kings Men.' They are both finding it easier to adopt an English turn of phrase when they choose to be overheard.

Chairs are being moved and sets installed noiselessly, actors are calm, none are having a nervous fit, it is a most unnatural state of a pre-performance order.

The King and Queen are guided to their rich velvet, throne-like chairs; padded footstools are placed nearby; a jewelled goblet of French claret is placed in the King's outstretched fingers. Select courtiers remain, some questioning internally whether they are indeed one of the 'select'. No one gets too close to the Royal couple, but behind there is a certain amount of jostling. They choose seats and order food. The Queen is utterly happy, her whole life has waited for this display for an audience, just like the old days in Denmark.

'Look,' she says pointedly to James, 'this is no' a birthin', no' a hingin' – it's a crowd of folk present to watch the floorishing of talent. God's gifts at work in our players.'

The King stares at the woman who is his wife, his Queen, and for a moment, before the play begins, he allows a sigh of admiration.

Fourteen

Forgive us our debts
as we forgive our debtors

Striding up and down in the morning light, in a padded yellow doublet and hose, arms behind his back, wearing a new hat jewel with four huge stones: diamond, ruby, emerald and pearl, James greets the day and greets Cecil, who he knows will support all he thinks.

'Was that no' a splendid night, my Beagle? Whit a play, whit felicitous plays on words, jeux des mots, what handsome players and dresses. Sic a nicht is fit for a king, and I am a king, let us no' forget.' He is ecstatic. 'What is his name, the Makar?'

'William Shakespeare, your Majesty.'

'Decorate him, decorate them all. Gie them red velvet robes.'

'May I gently remind your Majesty that you inherited not only our blessed late Queen's kingdom but also her debts.'

'How much?'

'£350,000 – which has doubled since your arrival.'

'Doubled in two years, not bad. Tell me of a king who was niver in debt. And are we no' well worth it?' James replies, and adds,

'Away Cecil, I will have no more talk of debt, it mars my appeteet and the Queen will have her jeweller. What becomes a king more than his jewels? Look, this new hatpin, it's worth more than your one castle at Theobalds?'

On his modest black, velvet hat is a brooch of monstrous proportions carrying a huge table diamond, a big ruby to the left, two glistening diamonds cut from the Great Harry jewel given to James' mother by Henri of France, two large pearls fixed on the head and diamonds studded around.

'A splendid decoration indeed, and who conceived of it?' asks Cecil.

'My own Scots jeweller, Heriot. It being a political piece, called The Mirror of Great Britain. The four precious jewels are the four kingdoms of Scotland, England, Ireland and Wales. Scotland is at the top, of course.'

'Of course...of course? What? Why not England, we provide the wealth.'

James is quick with his riposte, 'Aye, but we provide the brains, the leadership and the ingine. What use a rudderless ship, however laden with riches?'

'There is nothing more wonderful than your hat jewel, Majesty, but allow me to raise the money to pay for it.'

'Do that, my Beagle, and you shall have another palace more splendid than the first. And you shall call it Hatfield.'

'Your Majesty is full of wit.'

'Better than being full of schit.'

Cecil does not like James' ready and rude jokes, nor his casual habit of letting anyone approach him. Cecil is used to the deified Virgin Queen, whom he always addressed on his knees. She called him her 'wise little hunchback' or 'my pygmy' – there was something endearing in that. James now calls Cecil his 'Beagle', after the dog with short legs. He is loyal as a dog, that is true. But heavens, more dignified, with an education that put him through Westminster Parliament before he was twenty, Cambridge University, Europe to study law and languages and Flanders for experience in war. Refined, artistic, he has a horror of bloodshed and swearing and all things soldiersome. A lover of peace: at least this he shares with his King James.

And acute intelligence: James can see this and puts it to use.

'Though you are a little man, we shall load your shoulders with business.'

And Cecil knows exactly how to reply: 'His Majesty is the wisest of men: an angel messenger sent from Heaven.'

Layers of flattery too fine to be believed, though James does know he is on the throne through Divine Plan.

Nonetheless, courtiers distrust Cecil's physical deformities as much as they distrust James' limp and strong Scots accent. They are lepers together.

'Is it too early for breakfast, my Beagle?'

Cecil leaves briskly and a page enters with fruits, breads and an egg.

James takes the egg and commands, 'Porridge, my good lad, ask for porridge.'

The boy stands dismayed, then leaves with Cecil, who explains what porridge is.

Nearby, in a humbler but still beautiful dwelling, in the parish of St Martin in the Fields, Christian Heriot lies on a carved wooden bed, which stands on clean stone flags. Over her is a fine patchwork quilt picked out in red embroidery and beneath her head a lace pillow. She stares ahead at the high diamond paned window.

George enters dressed in better cloth than he has ever had before and asks her how she is,

'Today I hae the wind for company,' she says, staring into the distance with her hollowed out eyes, her clean brown hair spread thinly on the pillow. She can feel the softness of the blanket beneath her body and knows she is no longer poor, but it is too late. She closes her lids, ignoring George.

Rachel comes close and explains to him, 'She is mad with grief, sire. It is as though her mind is flayed, she is so delicate that the fold of a leaf or the shadow of a moth can make her twitch and weep, and she cries out for her Johnny and Geordie.'

George kneels by the bed and strokes her head, holding her hand to push strength into the limp and unfeeling body. She tries to turn and look at him but the tears well up and she cries, wretched.

'You'll mend soon enough, Christian, then we'll go and visit some braw new freens of mine in the jewel district in the city. You will like it, it's fu' o' life.'

Life, however, is draining out of Christian, quickly by the hour.

Heriot orders an expensive doctor, highly recommended by an English Lord at court, because he is desperate. The doctor bleeds Christian from both arms, which weakens her further and the inevitable happens: she slips away without a murmur, uncomplaining to the last breath, light in her death.

George goes out into the teeming London street, walking fast in any direction, blinded by his tears and driven by the anger at his God. Up an alley he finds a hard wall to punch again and again with his bare fist till blood breaks through the knuckles. A head appears at a window above.

'How now, good sir, that's my wall you are about to destroy.'

George glances at his raw fist and, mesmerised, licks the blood from it.

'What ails you my friend?' asks the head from the window. 'Come up and share a drink with me.' When his request is met with silence, the young man descends and approaches George in the alley.

'Christopher, I am Christopher, and you, sir?'

George falls and blacks out. He revives shortly with a kindly face leaning over him and offering him a drink from a flask. It is a strong drink, making him splutter.

'Potato wine, sir. I make it myself.' Christopher smiles.

'Where am I?' asks George.

'London, this is London.'

George sits up. 'You English are not so bad after all.'

Christopher has a quick laugh and flashing eyes. 'Maybe they're not. But I am Irish, I come from Donegal, and where are you from?'

'Edinburgh. But my wife has died in this damn place. She shouldna hae left the auld country.'

'Dead, is she? Well man, she'll be in a better place than this now, won't she? Come.'

He lifts George up off the street and leans him against the wall.

'Will ye no come up to my rooms?'

Not even potato wine can tempt him. George thanks him and declines.

He finds his own way home and is inconsolable for weeks, until he receives a letter from his own father in Edinburgh, who quotes a local poet, William Drummond:

'Death is not painful or evil, except in contemplation of the cause, being of itself as indifferent as Birth…Death is but a short, nay sweet, sigh.'

George keeps this page in his coat pocket for the rest of his days. It is as valuable as the letters documenting the debts that keep accruing from his royal patrons.

Fifteen

Rex Pacificus King of Peace

'One million four hundred thousand pounds, your Majesty.'

'What is that for, my Beagle? Shall we buy Spain?'

'No, sire, that is our national debt, and it is mounting as we speak.'

'How can it mount as we speak? I'm not buying anything, I'm not at war. Mine is a glorious peace, I am Rex Pacificus, the King of peace.'

'Daily expenses, ambassadors all over the known world, new Palaces, Hatfield House, your hat jewels.'

'Magnificent are they not? And the Unknown World, can we have some ambassadors there too? But you can sort it can you not, my Beagle? My infinitely clever Treasurer?'

'And Lord Buckingham.'

'Yes, I wantit to ask you aboot that. Can you gie him 20,000 pounds?'

'He is already wearing more than that sum about his clothing.'

'I hae made hat jewels a fashion.'

'And leg jewels, and rings.'

The Lord Treasurer is silent for a moment, then knows what he will do.

'It is such a nice day, what about a lunch party at Theobalds House and the morning spent hunting through the woods en route?'

Delighted, the King always accepts any suggestion of a hunt, particularly if it means that the day's business will be postponed. Robert Cecil goes on ahead of the party to prepare the household for the royal visit. They spend half a day riding through woodland in good company, and after it, are both sweating and thirsty. Cecil asks the King to follow him to a locked chamber.

Inside it is dark, the shutters and curtains are drawn, the room is lit by only one large, branched candelabra on a vast oak table in the centre. Piled onto the table are heaps and heaps of silver coins, all counted out in piles, glinting in the light, newly minted.

James is embarrassed at this vulgar display.

'What is that?' he asks awkwardly.

'That is the 20,000 you wish to give Buckingham.'

James is aghast. He approaches the table and moves back before touching it.

'Three thousand is enough.'

Cecil has plans for saving money that no one else can imagine: selling crown properties, selling titles, raising taxes, handing over customs duties to parliament to look after.

In the ruling of a country, someone has to rise and someone has to fall: it happens quickly, quietly, daily. Decisions are made every second. Cecil is the man who can manage the King and link him to Parliament.

But to interrupt Cecil's saving schemes with an extravagant display of hospitality, the Danish King Christian IV arrives in mid-July to visit his sister, Queen Anne. She has not seen her dear brother since her childhood, her happy childhood when she was brought up at the same court as her parents and siblings. Now he visits to see her triumphant as queen of a wealthy country and mother of three live children and more on the way. Courtiers who last week were told to keep austerity, now hear every day the sounds of trumpets, hautboys, music, revels and comedies.

On the 5th August there is jousting. Trumpeters in green with shining instruments hung with tapestries announce the Challenge of the Errant Knights before the palace gate of Greenwich. The challengers offer to maintain by all the allowed ways of knightly arguing – meaning by lance and sword, four indisputable propositions in praise of Love and Beauty.

King Christian, mounted on a dapple grey, wearing a shining sky-coloured suit of armour, spangled with gold, and with a bunch of blue and white plumes in his helmet, breaks some lancing staves with marvellous grace and great applause from the gathered people. The young poet William Drummond of Hawthornden is on a visit to London en route for the continent to study for the more sensible occupation of Law. He is watching the display in a crowd of courtiers, standing beside George Heriot who can't help explaining.

'Sky-blue enamel is very difficult to make, especially for a whole body-suit of armour.'

William hears the other members of the court remarking:

'But he's rich, sire, rich: Denmark has an Empire, like Rome did.'

'Fine work. And that blue plume, what bird is that?'

'An Ostrich, must be the Ostrick.'

'Fool! They are not blue.'

'He must be hot in the sun.'

'Watch him go.'

The horse, a glistening muscled beast, charges forward and the knight hits his opponent flat on the shield with a loud bang and knocks him off his horse. It is William Herbert, Earl of Pembroke.

'Good for Pembroke.'

'Wise to allow the Queen's brother to win.'

'He did win.'

King Christian dismounts and Heriot spots none other than Lady Marjorie, his terrifying in-law, fresh from Edinburgh, now bustling up to the triumphant King. What possible pretext has she?

Marjorie beams, 'A message from your sister, Majestie.'

Marjorie is not one of Anna's ladies in waiting, but the Danish King Christian does not know this. Marjorie is still a force to command an audience and she spends time with the Queen and Prince Charles.

George does not have the sheer smeddum required to approach a foreign monarch and curious, moves forward to try and hear what she is saying.

Marjorie lifts her thick embroidered skirts clear of the mud churned by horses' hooves but keeps her eye on the prize. The King, like everyone else, is drawn to her magnificent bosom, displayed to best advantage beneath the flame-red hair, ready smile and calculating gaze, a gaze that reflects, closes, flirts, changes, engages, locks – all within a fraction of a second. King Christian is hooked. Turning his back on the ambassador, he links arms with the lady, and they wander off together, leaving Heriot at a loss behind not catching up, not hearing the intimate exchange of two heads bent towards each other, smiling, laughing, enjoying their own company. At once George feels himself to be the lesser courtier. How does she do it? She arrives at court three years late and instantly hooks the biggest fish.

They chat for five long minutes and part.

Turning, Marjorie passes George with a glowing face and patronizing tone, 'Heriot, my countryman, so you are here too!'

'Aye Lady Marjorie, I have been here these past three years too. And yourself, come to jine us?'

Marjorie flushes and keeps a six-foot distance. 'Indeed,' she agrees, not giving details.

'And your wife? Christian?'

The words like stones wither Heriot. He looks at the mud on the hem of her dress.

'I am so sorry,' she gushes, and glides effortlessly on.

Heriot again hears the voices of the courtiers around him.

'They will see Love's Labour Lost tonight.'

'Again?'

'It is the King's favourite play because of its title, he makes the same joke every time, about his seed, you must remember to laugh.'

Young William of Hawthornden suspects as wrong the cynicism of his companions. He came to see his father, now knighted, though not expected to joust, and his uncle, the Queen's secretary. And so he is allowed the freedom of the court. He has a simple unadulterated faith in his monarch and writes a letter home as they leave, which proves that he has also mastered the English turn of phrase: 'None of our pleasures are lasting; they, as all human things, have their end. The King of Denmark, the 9th of this month, taking leave of his sister and His Majesty (who with tears in their eyes returned) went towards his ships to Gravesend and has departed leaving a general commendation in this island of his virtues.'

Not only that, but King Christian has left a competitive thirst for empire. James says he also has an empire and decides to draw a flag which will unite his kingdoms, he will call it Jacobus after himself. Cecil names it the Union Jack, but it is not popular in any of the kingdoms.

***

George often walks alone now through the woods north to Highgate, early in the morning there is no one on the roads. Ahead he can see Christian as she used to be, stopping and stooping, she looks at a small, light bundle on the path, a nest, blown from a tree-top. It is exquisite with twisted strands of moss, fine long horsehairs of three colours, down feathers and sheep's wool, a bed for nestlings. She holds it, cupping two hands together in a gesture of benediction, gently nursing the birds' lost home, now on a path to be trampled. Taking it carefully she examines the trees around looking upwards and sideways, to the left is a group of three old yews, one of them dangerously tall, thin and creaking in the wind. It is too tall and thin for a yew and spindly it bends to the breeze, doubtless the nest fell from there. It will not go back up. Helpless and cradling the nest she tucks it into a curve in the trunk of an older thicker and stabler tree.

George runs to reach her but of course she is not there, he walks off the path around the clump of yews and finds the nest tucked by someone into the trunk, or did the wren build it there?

He crouches on the bank, hands over his eyes, overcome with grief.

Sixteen

The Reformation is over

'The Reformation is over, your Majesty,' says the Bishop of Oxford.

'The Reformation will niver be over. Not in these Isles. We will niver stint arguing aboot the Bible and all within. So long as one man sees hisel' as above his fellow man, then we will always reform the Church, till it ceases to exist at all.'

Andrew Melville and seven Calvinist compatriots have recently come from Scotland to explain the violence happening in the name of religion.

'And what are they complaining about now in Scotland?' asks the bishop.

'They do not like the words of the marriage vow in the Book of Common Prayer.'

'Which words?'

"With my body I thee worship." It is idolatry.'

'But withoot these wurds we shall beget no bairns, my Lord Melville,' bursts in James.

'The idea comes from the Whore of all Nations, my Lord, it is Catholic.'

'Even worse, it is heathenish, popish, Jewish and Arminian.'

'Dinna be daft. You, Melville, are the man who in Edinburgh called me 'God's sillie vassal'. Now wha's bein sillie?'

The King is closeted with the dark-dressed, sour-mouthed Presbyterians for up to an hour. Then he quietly whispers to his Treasurer who whispers to the guard and they are all taken politely to the Tower of London where they will remain as guests of his Majesty for the next three years,

'For being silly and to keep them out of mischief.' Says the Fool.

'They are weel treatit,' replies the King.

'The doors are heavy, the guards are good, the walls are thick.'

'I askit you for some revelrie,' warns James.

The Fool puts on his three-pronged velvet hat with bells and shakes his stick, which has a small skull at the end. He turns back flips and handstands and everyone watches including the King. Then he grabs apples from the fruit bowl and juggles with increasing numbers and skill until at twelve he drops them. Picking them up apologetically he hands them to a woman servant who has entered and says,

'A few bruises, but they will still make a pie, Clemence.'

Clemence is still and blond and rounded, she appears sane and healthy. Holding out her apron she looks the wiry and nervous Fool in the eye and thanks him. He takes succor from the stare, and continues bravely to say,

'The Scots have balls, your Majesty. You'll never break them, but you can soften them.'

James is jolted into an idea of his own, one discussed before with Cecil and voiced again now by Cecil: 'They don't understand you, your Majesty, and they would if they visited and stayed more often...Every Scots nobleman should send his sons to England to be educated. That must be law. They will learn the ways of the state that governs them. They will get good jobs at Court. And we will castrate a rebellion before it even starts.'

The Fool does a little dance, with more apples, and some lewd gestures.

'By grabbing your jewels, you soften their balls...'

'Enough,' says the King, turning to his small chancellor.

James starts talking to Cecil, who, lifting his arm with its heavy sleeves carefully so that the folds do not land on the King's lap, passes him a letter to sign and a quill with which to sign it, taking it from a table where his secretary is organizing the ink and sand for dusting.

'Here I sit and govern Scotland with my pen when others couldna do it with the sword,' announces James.

The Fool, only momentarily distracted, hears the King's clever saying, and concludes,

'So you will not execute these Scotsmen in the Tower.'

In spite of Cecil's disapproving glance, the Fool continues in poetic style,

'Words are precious like water

Words are precious like sunlight'

***

Meanwhile George is sitting in sunlight, writing at his large oak table in his airy hall with the high glass windows. The dog is lying in a patch of sun on the floor and lifts head and tail together as George shifts his foot. Rachel is cleaning the floor with a wet cloth tied onto a broom. She carefully circumnavigates the wolfhound who stares ahead masterfully.

George looks up, 'I am going to marry again.'

Rachel looks pleased, 'Good, my Lord.'

'I shall go to collect her from Edinburgh. I may be gone a month.'

It is 1608 and George longs for his homeland: the narrow wynds, the grey skies and the unforgiving wind; his own house in Fishmarket Close, the Grassmarket looking up at the Castle frowning, glowering on its dominating rock. And the light so bright it shakes you. The view of the sea from the Royal Mile. The apple trees in the gardens, not that there aren't apple trees in London; he found some on a walk to Highgate village.

But the visit to Edinburgh disappoints him. He is no longer remembered. 'Ye leave fur a year an ye're deid,' says a fishwife in the Close. Even the beggars are different; a younger lot he notices ominously – a life on the street is a short one. George has been gone six years and now Christian is dead. George's relatives have kindly introduced by letter and suggested a new wife – a young one because, like the beggars, a life of childbearing is also a short one.

The pretty and accomplished Alison is sixteen and she knows enough to hide her fear of him. Her parents are well aware of the opportunity offered for a link with the Heriot family, and marriage to a man so highly-placed at court. It is apparent to them that Heriot is kindly and understanding, not old and lecherous, even if he is forty-seven. This will unite his Scottish interests with his London job. He wants to return to Edinburgh to retire one day. He is setting a precedent for others to come, getting a good job in London and sending the money home.

'Dinna breed her into the ground,' Advises his new father-in-law of Alison. George knows what that means: his own cousin Grizel has nineteen children and is a cussed and cantankerous wumman, always in need of money for her brood. George has money and he gives freely. But what will he not give for some bairns of his own? Grizel will have to lend some of her children.

He takes Grizel's two eldest sons back to London, one as a secretary and the other an apprentice. George can see the irony, as they are far more of an age to marry Alison than he is. But now he is like a mini monarch himself, with his considerable wealth and position. He checks every now and again that they are not flirting through the windows of the carriage as they ride south. They would not dare to, religious boys, they do not even admit to themselves that Alison is pretty and attractive, and she, even more prayerful, keeps her eyelids modestly lowered. Nonetheless the excitement of the journey, the smell of the adventure of riding all the way to London and to court makes the boys lively and full of energy, like new horses at a new race, and their own steeds feel it in the squeezes from their loins. A brightness in the eye from sheer enjoyment of exploration is infectious. It's not raining anymore and the road is dry. The wind blows away the last night's shower. The woods are alive with birdsong and deer, as Alison's fear evaporates and she can understand these two Edinburgh youths with their light-hearted yelps on Heriot's fresh horses. There is even a dog following, belonging to Horace, the older boy, and it sniffs around the earth and bounces back and fore covering more ground than it needs.

They stop for the night in Durham and see the cathedral rising vast and inhuman from the town. Never have they beheld such a building made by man. They circle it curiously and stare up at the carvings and the smashed stone faces of the figures on the outside, longing to go inside, but afraid, as they know it has been cleansed from idolatry and the stained-glass windows smashed by the reformers of the Church.

Back on the road the next day it is such good weather that they stop at midday and sit on a bank overlooking the road, eating their bannocks and cheese, and sipping wine, as yet a new taste, passed round by George. They are sitting on dry oak leaves in comfortable piles; when suddenly from beneath a bank of leaves, a child emerges. He is a dirty, mad-looking, thin thing in rags with a face covered in little cuts; half-starved, he approaches Alison who at once gives him her bread.

George steps near to keep the child away from his wife.

'Dinna touch him. He looks diseased. Speak up boy, what ails ye?'

The boy opens his mouth and points inside. His tongue has been cut out. He goes down on his knees and makes a sign of the cross then puts his hand inside his pocket and pulls out a set of rosary beads. His clear intelligence in conveying his situation with a few brief gestures, is at odds with his wretched appearance, also his courage in displaying his religion to strangers.

George explains to his charges, 'They cut oot the tongues o' them that pray the rosary.'

'But so young? I have heard o' priests wi' tongues cut oot, no bairns.'

The boy listens and holds his rosary in his pocket.

George puts his hand in his own pocket and pulls out a small bag of coins. He takes out three gold coins and hands them to the child who cannot believe his luck, but looks quizzically at the jeweller.

'How will he buy things if he canna speak?' asks Alison, as George hands her back into the carriage and the group set off again on the road.

Excitement has worn off and a stunned silence reigns over the travellers. As if in response, the heavens open and the rest of the day gives torrential rain and grey skies. Alison now shares the carriage with the dog, which licks her hand and paws her dress. Horace shouts through the carriage window and the dog lies still, steaming and smelling.

Nottingham is the final stop before London and the inn is crowded with wet cloaks and the stable with hungry horses. George gets the boys to look after the animals, while he and his new wife eat together in a small private room with their bed. Alison, timid and tired from the day, eats little then she turns her face to the wall and sleeps.

George goes downstairs to check on the boys, who will bed down in the stable with the grooms. He takes them to the tavern and buys pork chops and potatoes on a heavy pewter plate, with small beer. He tells them not to discuss the beggar child they have seen that day, but to think on better things, to read their Bible and go to sleep because tomorrow is the last day of riding before London

He removes his boots thoughtfully beside his sleeping bride. Tonight is not the night for his marital duties, and he is half-feart for the outcome: he does not want to lose another wife.

Seventeen

The Masque of Beauty
and a bauble for a Prince

'How is your new wife, George?' asks Anna, 'You rode to win her from Scotland. Gey far to gang for a wife, when I could have found one for you here.'

'Not so far, considering you were won from Denmark, your Majestie, further still. I remember it well. Transported over the cobbles fae Leith in a silver carriage, and the fountains ran wi' wine.'

'We'll have a celebration for the new Mistress Heriot. Will you bring her?'

Heriot bows, 'Of course.'

'And she shall take part in a Masque.'

Heriot is slightly alarmed. Anna's Masques are the very opposite of Scottish Presbyterian thinking – lavish extravagance with high cost and some nakedness.

'I have a new one being written by Jonson called the Masque of Beauty. Inigo Jones is designing and a new composer scrieving the music.'

Heriot hears that the last Masque, the Masque of Blackness, cost over £100,000 – enough to build a palace, or educate the whole of Edinburgh. He might do both with that money.

Anna continues, 'For this Masque, half of the performers shall all be paintit in blackness as if the skin is dark, the rest shall be pure or white. Your wife shall be a pure one. How old is she?'

'Sixteen.'

'A ripe age for being in a Masque.' Queen Anna continues, 'You ken it is also the occasion of opening the new feasting hall at the Palace of Whitehall.'

Alison is timid and young and will not perform in a Masque, Heriot knows – but how to get around this one? Not the whole Court seeing her in transparent silk, for heaven's sake.

'She has a cough, Majestie.' A pretty lame excuse, but he can give her a cough.

'Bring her to Court. She shall see the Masque with you.'

That was easy.

He walks home through the streets, oblivious to the mud and sea of faces in the dark afternoon along by the Thames. Now, to get her dressed. George knows he can leave that to Rachel, who has daughters of her own who are Alison's age.

Entering and handing over his cloak, he says to Rachel, 'Alison has been invitit to Court. Can ye find a dress maker?'

'The best dressmaker at Court has been found to be a poisoner, and executed.'

Heriot is silently shocked. Absorbed by book-keeping, business and jewel-making, he never listens to Court gossip.

'Then the second-best dressmaker will not be a poisoner. We are safe,' he concludes.

The second-best dressmaker gilds the lily George has wed in Scotland. She is almost unrecognizable and not entirely comfortable, her tiny waist exaggerated by the vast dress: lace, velvet brocade, silk, hair, jewels all vying for attention and the small, faint-hearted Alison trying to rise to the occasion.

She protests at the jewels in her hair. 'Please George, can we no gie them to the poor?'

He is proud of her. 'A true Protestant maks plaint.' He takes the jewel and puts it back on her hair. 'Wear it tonight, and the morn I promise we gie the money to the poor.'

'Yon bairn we saw by the weyside wi' no parents. Can we gie money tae faitherless bairns?'

'Aye, lass.' George kisses her. 'But mak me proud o ye the night, Alison. Stand straight, look beautiful, curtsey to their Majesties, say little, and watch the Masque.'

The Palace of Whitehall is vast beyond imaginings and the Masque is long, glittering, with elaborate music and jewelled costumes, embroidered in real gold. Each of the hundreds of chairs sat on by the audience have miniature paintings of Dutch pastoral scenes with windmills in the background: all different.

The words and the songs are worth listening to:

'Had those that dwell in error foul

And hold that women have no soul,

But seen these move, they would have then

Said women were the souls of men.

So they do move each heart and eye

With the world's soul, true harmony.'

At the end, a handsome well-bedecked courtier approaches the Heriots and asks to be presented to Alison.

'Ben Jonson writes these things to please the Queen, otherwise he will get no more work; he doesn't believe them.'

'But do you believe them, my Lord Pembroke?' asks George.

'What? That women have no soul?'

'Jonson is contesting that.'

Alison bursts in, 'Women have far more soul than men and can be corrupted too.'

She is thinking of the poisoner.

'More soul? I like a competition. You my lady prove beyond doubt that a deep and feeling soul exists. But, a greater one? Tell me, do.'

Alison is getting flustered and George comes swiftly to help, leading her gently away from the flirtatious Lord with his tights and short padded breeches, which show off his shapely legs.

Instinctively Alison feels that there is something wrong with the excess in gowns and breeches, cloaks and hats, though it keeps dressmakers in income, and her husband and all his apprentices in work. She is amazed that there are so many dogs wandering around at the ball. It is the opening of the new banqueting hall, and the floor is strewn with flowers; among them the sleek, small hounds and pretty lapdogs sniff each other as avidly as their masters and mistresses flirt higher up.

Alison was not born to preen like these ladies of the Court. Though not much older than her, they sport the stiffened jewelled clothes, tight stays, padded sleeves, ruffs and petted dogs of the very rich. They are brought up to it, have servants to ensure it all functions, and are actors in a show of wealth. The flirtation itself is not even for pleasure, as marriage is a necessity. It is a necessity for the parents who wish to form an alliance with another family, or heal a rift, or for the nakedly ambitious, to socially climb. To Pembroke and Buckingham it seems odd that someone with the wealth, position and influence of George Heriot should not choose a wife from the ranks of the nobles when he could do so easily.

'Instead the cussed man rides all the way to Edinburgh for a wee Scots lassie, sixteen years old, mind, who canna thole the life here,' intones Buckingham.

Pembroke corrects him, 'Instead the ill-advised gentleman rides to Edinburgh for a small girl of sixteen years who cannot sustain a life at Court.'

Buckingham retorts, 'Thole is not sustain. Thole is bear; she canna bear it – look at her…'

Alison, whose ears are better than they think, is blushing to mirror her red gown, and is acutely aware of her tight lacing beneath the layers and the sharp pointed stomacher that emphasizes her slim waist. She is so unnerved by this new lush life that she has not bled for three months now. Or is that why she has not bled? She is eating properly though some foods make her want to throw up. A tray of sweets in the shape of all the fishes and shells of the sea is flashed before her by a page boy dressed like Poseidon. He is the age of her younger brother, perhaps ten, and her longing for a simple life at home overwhelms her.

'Is that tray heavy?'

'No,' lies the child, sweating and breathing hard. 'Take a sweet, ladyship. All the fruits of the sea, but sweets.'

In order to lighten his burden, Alison chooses the heaviest-looking oyster shell. The boy passes on, grateful. She cannot eat such a huge glut of sweetmeat, and offers it to her husband. He, bewildered, takes it from her and eats slowly, watching the pageantry before them.

There are five hundred people in the room including servants and armed guards, clergy, foreign ambassadors and guests. Most numerous are the decorated courtiers, and George can spot his workmanship on display. He has made hat jewels a fashion, and everyone copies the King and the King only wears Heriot's work. Heriot is well pleased – to a certain extent.

The great hall has been divided in two by a wooden partition, carved elaborately, about waist height. On one side are scaffolds of raked seating and making for it are the audience, which George and Alison join, climbing to get a good view of the stage below. Guests flow in through the double doors: greying, bearded, coated, hatted, hand in hand, smiling, open-mouthed, be-wigged, be-trousered and be-trewed, with patent leather gloves and shoes; one carries a hawk, hooded, on his arm.

George is astonished again to spot Lady Marjorie among them, he cannot miss her. Her skill at talking is unsurpassed; she can work through a room, even a ballroom in Whitehall, without dropping her dog or her champagne glass. Her dog is small and yappy but quiet when under her arm, eyes lovingly and jealously focused on Marjorie but inclined to snap at the young chiels who venture to seek her favours. Marjorie's favours are not sexual, she does not make that mistake, they are social, and by that meaning much more powerful.

On her left Alison feels the bony elbows of the elderly Duchess of Blander. After the age of fifty a woman's knowledge and experience of life give her the power of manipulation, insinuation, gossip and also, on the good side, protection and advice. The Duchess' wig, heavy with a pearl brooch that swings near to Alison's head, smells of lavender and age as though it has been sitting in a box all year waiting for this outing, which of course it has. Alison's hair is her own, but her thoughts are unsure as the Duchess speaks,

'Congratulations on your marriage, Mistress Heriot. You are the talk of the Court.'

Alison looks embarrassed and alarmed.

'Why?'

'Your jewels will rival the Queen's.'

'Surely no'.'

'What a man will not give to the woman he loves…'

George Heriot leans over his wife to reply to the Duchess and warn her not to make such jokes that may alarm his young bride.

The show begins: to the sound of trumpets and drums the King, Queen, Prince Charles and Princess Elizabeth enter, processing to their own raised canopy surrounded by their acolytes. Most magnificent of all is Prince Henry in a leather doublet, short tight-fitting hose and crimson velvet livery with broad gold lace. Dressed like a gilded Roman centurion, on his head sits an eagle shaped helmet with gigantic ostrich feathers. And here he shows his martial arts.

Attendants clatter out with burnished weapons, shields and banners to the middle of the room. Youths of Court, Henry's age and experience, now set to and fight it out by the rules using swords and sixteen-foot pikes. Blow for blow and aggressive crash for crash, Henry never leaves the floor all evening. With vigour and skill he shows his father that he has now come of age, at fifteen he is man and prince in waiting for kingship.

This is a night to remember and the Court do not ignore its significance.

Alison however does not understand. George explains to her that it is a play fight, but she is faint with sitting still and listening to clatters and bangs, she begs to go home. George is relieved. As soon as the throng permits, they are outside in the fresh air and not far from their home near St Martin in the Fields. He hands her into the carriage, she leaning heavily on his arm.

Next day, Rachel informs Alison that she must be pregnant, because she has not had her bleeding for three months. Alison asks how she Rachel could know that.

'I wash your undergarments, Madam. There is little I do not know.'

***

Queen Anne, for she is Anne in England and, as her name changes, her speech must also, is sitting in her half-built theatre set for the next Masque. The half that is built is splendid, ordered, measured, calm, restful on the eye with views to the distance of a river and green hills.

The presence of dozens of builders constructing the unfinished half gives it all an air of artist's work in progress, a busy-ness, a depth. Anna's favourite, Inigo Jones, is on site discussing plans with the chief builders and painters. He approaches his Queen to explain,

'The trompe l'oeiul paysage. I must explain every detail, every tiny detail. I cannot leave them to build it alone, your Majesty.'

Anna is watching him talk to the painters working on a climbing rose bush, still in orange flower, but dense enough to hide behind. She is fascinated by the work but does not want to understand the detail.

'And whose idea is this?'

'Mine, your Majesty. But I want to go to Italy to study buildings, and then build palaces. One great man, Palladio, who's book I obtained in Italian, died not long ago, but I would do anything to see his works.'

As if from nowhere, unannounced, Lady Marjorie appears.

'How can ye stay here, Majestie, with all this dust and noise?' She pronounces noise as two words, 'No Ease.'

Jones looks offended.

'Lady Marjorie', Anna smiles, 'the Prince Charles and I are waiting for you.'

She leads the way to her rooms in the palace quickly, Marjorie hurrying to catch up. There, Charles is sitting completely at ease on a low chaise longue with two puppies on his lap, one of them attempting to clean the long princely hair with her tongue.

'What a bonnie, natural boy, what a blythe soul,' exclaims Marjorie, 'It is almost as if he would mak a better king.'

Anna is taken aback by Marjorie's ability to divine her closest thoughts and feelings.

'It's true. I barely see Henry now, but he is over-eddicatit, too much math and military strategy. He has designed his own war already.'

'Charles prefers people and nature and art – the humanities. He's more like his mother, and more at ease with religion.'

'But today is the day for his jewel,' asserts Anna.

It is one of Heriot's few remaining visits to Anna; they have become fewer with each busier working year. He has no idea that Marjorie is part of a plot, or even her own plot, for plots go on all the time, day and night, and the plotters are often unaware themselves. It is simply the expression of a wish or the observation of an idea. Marjorie's plot might be called treason.

Anna greets him as he is already in the room, 'My auld Scots freens.' For she switches between language and words as befits the occasion.

Laughing and clapping her hands as she used to as a child, 'Now for some joy! A hat jewel for Charles, George – and it must be braw!'

Marjorie takes the idea and runs on, 'Grand. A jewel with ambition – like the Mirror of Britain you made for the King. A star to shine over Charles' head.'

Charles sits up at once, pushing off the dogs.

'No, I will not wear a hat jewel. That's for old men. I want a great earring – the greatest earring of all.'

Marjorie lapses, 'Yer faither detests hingers fur luggies.'

Charles' eyes light up, 'Quite so, master Heriot, make it big!'

'Hingers fur luggies are worn by some of the King's best favourites, the most fashionable men at court; Buckingham and Villiers…' suggests George.

Marjorie interrupts, 'Buckingham, ha. That vogie, he's awbody's body.'

'Yes, a grand earring,' Charles ignores Marjorie and turns to Heriot, jumping off the couch and standing up excited.

Heriot thinks for a moment, then addresses himself to Anna, 'This can be a special one. I have found a pearl of great price, the largest ever seen; like a linnet's egg, and on its top, near the ear, I will build a crown, a monarch's crown, to signify your royal blood.'

'Or kingship,' suggests Marjorie, 'a crown for kings.'
Heriot replies steadily, 'Princes also wear crowns.'

Eighteen

1612 – Snow like wool, frost like ashes

Alison and George are sitting together at the circular oak table in their hall. There is a large leather-bound Bible before them. Alison reads haltingly but with energy, following George's finger,

'He gives snow like wool: he scatters the hoarfrost like ashes. He sends hailstanes like crumbs – who can withstand his cold?'

She stops and looks at him.

'That's good, Alison, you're a real student.'

His wife stares ahead, 'Bytimes frost looks like ashes, but mainly, when the sun is on it in the morn, it's like diamonds. It's better than diamonds.'

'God's warld is better than a king's. Though ye canna compare ower much. He made diamonds too, for his ain raison. But it is man that warks them and maks them glitter; an unwarked stone is rough and clarty.'

George puts his hand in his pocket and brings out his little leather purse held with a drawstring. He opens it flat and shows an uncut diamond, dull like a piece of melted glass.

'Then your apprenteeces get to wark on it.'

'Man's wark. And I thank God for it.'

He collects the little stones together carefully and hands one to Alison.

'Now whit would ye dae wi' that?'

His sixteen-year-old wife looks excited and suddenly gets a lightness in her eye. She throws the diamond up into the air and catches it, to tease him. Then throws it up and catches it in her mouth. George cannot believe the audacity, but is smiling at her play,

'Don't swallow...'

Too late, she is not in control of the throat when giggling. Her eyes widen. She opens her mouth. 'I am sairy.'

She breathes, upset, 'Oh, I'm vext.'

George bends over with laughter. He cannot control himself, tears flow and she takes her cue, soon also crying with mirth. George falls off the chair and Rachel comes in.

'She's swallowed a diamond.' He explains, rising.

Rachel slowly assessing the situation, but ever practical says, 'It's alright. It will pass through, if you eat some bread.'

She exits and returns with a basket of bread, while George recovers, closes the Bible and puts his stones carefully back into their purse.

Alison dutifully picks up a piece of dry bread. George watches her.

'Rachel,' he calls, 'Bring us some red wine for the bread,' he thinks again, 'And some cheese.' He sits down again.

He has now truly fallen in love.

Rachel returns, carrying a tray with a jug of wine, pewter goblets, a cheese and some apples.

George dips a piece of bread in the red wine and offers it to Alison who takes it, looking into his eyes.

That afternoon, he does not go back to work.

George arrives late in the workshop, humming to himself. He stands in the window and allows the last of the sunlight to land through the diamond shaped panes on his padded jacket, outside he can see the holly tree has red berries. It will soon be Christmas.

At last he will be given a child as a present. What more could anyone wish for? Gold, Diamonds, treasure? He has always had enough of these and they were never anything he desired, they are simply work. But he discovers there is work too in nourishing the woman who will bring forth his child. The correct servants, some visits from relations in Edinburgh, pleasing the relatives enough to please his wife: everything to please that sacred vessel that carries his child.

Having lost both wife and children before, he is solicitous to the last detail this time round.

'No, you canna visit Edinburgh. Traivel is bannit in your condition. Edinburgh will come to you.'

The house is transformed for the comfort of Alison's mother and sister who arrive by four-day journey in a rattling coach over rutted roads. Both are ill from the journey on arrival and Alison cares for them herself with the help of Rachel, who asks George for another two servants. Now everyone has a servant, and food, bedding and clothing for the household increase. George thinks it wise to rent the house next door, and moves there with his desk and books and the dog so as to leave more room for Alison and her ladies.

Alison misses her husband and visits him next door.

'When will ye retour to oor bed, George?'

'When there's room. It is most important that you are cared for and rested and the child is safe.'

'But this is more tiring. It was better just oorsels and Rachel. Now there's mair mooths to feed and I mak deceesion fur meals, and sometimes she doesna want it…'

'Who?'

'Mither. Yestreen the cook cookit an aiple tairt, so brawly cut and arrainged, she had warked on it a' efternoon. She haundelt a dainty ashet to us a' at the table and mither jist makit a face – an ungratefu' face – and shuved it away. But I pretendit it hadna happenit and haivered aw ither thing.

They're ayways askin' aboot fashions at court, so I telt them. But I'm wabbit wi their demands.'

'Now they are here, we canna exactly get shot o' them. Edinburgh is a long way away. We planned to hae them till the birthin.'

Alison sits down. George strokes her shoulder and face, and smiles.

'My ain mither is much worse, I'll warrant you.'

'Mithers. And I am aboot to become one.'

'It will be mony decades afore ye refuse the aiple tairt.'

Rachel knocks and enters with the offending tart. 'My Lord, I thought you…'

George laughs and he and Alison sit down to eat the tart on pewter plates, with a jug of thick cold cream. Alison eats with gusto.

She has to leave by an outdoor path through the small garden which has not been cleared of frost and snow. Lines of the psalms are always singing through her head as she walks, she repeats, 'snow like wool, frost like ashes…' and slips on the path.

No one hears her cry and she lies there silent and as if sleeping, until George lets the dog out to relieve itself. The dog bounds over to Alison's still form and whines.

Panic sets in. George cries,

'Alison, Alison,' He moves her shoulder. 'Rachel,' he howls. Mother and sister come to the door and rush over in the snow. Rachel appears and sends the male servant for a doctor. They carry Alison into her own house – dog, master, mother, sister and servant – and lay her on a couch. Rachel brings water for her brow. Her hands and lips are blue with cold, her skin paper-thin and white. Eyes slightly open but seeing nothing, and saying nothing.

'She breathes,' cries mother triumphantly.

The doctor arrives, the same one that bled Christian Heriot six years before.

Heriot balks. 'No, stop there. No further. Rachel, please find another doctor.'

Rachel protests that there is no other doctor that she knows of.

The doctor protests that he must bleed the patient quickly.

'No,' says George, 'leave her, I will nurse her myself.'

'Go, everyone leave.' He shouts, and they obey.

Like a precious jewel, he arranges the bed around her. Strokes her brow with his strong, sensitive fingers. Holds her hands and presses each finger as if testing a surface to be hewn. He pinches the gap between her thumb and fore finger and feels each of her digits as if it is a golden wire. His hands are his tools; they are gentle and loving just as the doctor's instruments are cruel and sharp. Next he massages her head and neck and shoulders in the way his groom does his horse, thoroughly with concentration. He is pushing the life back into her veins, warming her with his own warmth.

Alison wakes. Her cheeks and lips become pink, her eyelids move. 'George,' she whispers. 'Ye're here, I thocht I lost ye.'

It is a strange spring: brittle and clean as a virgin, with a hard purity. Snowdrops come and go and more snow with frost follows. Alison recovers but stays indoors resting. She is forbidden to go outside the door. George comes to visit her every evening and spends hours nursing her. He oversees her food and entertainment. She must read and play games and be merry. He wishes he could bring her to court to see the new plays by The Kings Men, but the air inside his home is sacrosanct, and she must not be exposed to the raging fevers that wander out of doors. He organizes scrupulous cleaning and polishing; changing of bedclothes, boiling of water and preparing of broth. There is porridge for breakfast, broth at midday and boiled meat and vegetables at dinner; often a tart with cream. He trusts no doctor.

When he goes to Court George hears that young Prince Henry is ill with the vapours. One of the many doctors called is his own and in an uncharacteristic move, George walks up to him and begs him not to advise bleeding.

At home Alison gets up early and takes a forbidden walk. Birdsong greets her and she walks at speed through the singing woods. The excitement makes the girl sweat and sit beneath a tree in a daze as Rachel hurries to catch up with her and brings her home before George hears of it. But he does and sits by her bed, listening to the delirious girl:

'Dew. I was telt they're faeries teardraps. Faeries onlie daunder at nicht when we're asleep. At creek o' day, they each greet a tear, so weary are they to leave the earth for faerie land again.'

Rachel, steady as always, consoles her, 'There are no faeries in England, dear.'

'No,' George agrees.

'It wis just what I was telt as a child.'

'You will have your own child soon.'

Alison's belly is rounded but not large. She is a slim nineteen-year-old and this is their third pregnancy, the last two slipped away early on. But Rachel says this is normal and not to be fretted over,

'Just eat well and enjoy what life God gives us. That is what Prince Henry does, and he is just your age, Mistress.'

Rachel's close friend is housekeeper at St James's Palace and the wonders of the Prince's household are always being relayed. He is strict and religious like Alison's own husband, rises early, exercises, works hard, has a glittering list of guests who are experts on his interests in science and mathematics, ships and machines, not to forget poets of all sorts.

Lady Marjorie is also one of the guests at Henry's court, she was invited for her knowledge of young people and who should marry who. It is said she gifted the Prince a priceless silk lace handkerchief wrought by a foreign princess, but will not reveal the name, and this has given the Prince great amusement through guessing.

'But of late his sheets are too rumpled with sweat.'

'Does he have a wife?' asks the innocent Alison.

'No, but the King insists and many are suggested. Catholics and Protestants. Whether to take a Catholic and unite the warring states of Europe or to marry a kindred spirit in a Protestant and have a mind like his own? That is the Prince's dilemma. And that, I warrant, is why he stays awake at night tortured with the thought.'

'And he cannot marry one he loves?'

'No, and nor did you my dear. But love grows.'

The sounds of a mother scolding her child in the street outside the window in harsh tones, then the high-pitched wail of the child, interrupt their conversation. Alison is affected, Rachel notices, with the same sensitivity as Christian when she was ill. Alison jumps at the child's cry with an expression of mortal pain.

'It's only a child, Mistress, small worries.'

Then as if on cue, there is a louder wailing, and this time not a child's, but the wailing of larger numbers of women, at first in the distance and then getting nearer, and frantic mutterings, then more wails. It is as if the whole of London is weeping.

Rachel rushes to the window, then to the outside door. She returns pale and terror struck.

'As I feared. Prince Henry is dead.'

Alison cannot believe it, but the wails continue.

George returns, bursting into the room with a rough, cream-coloured paper in his hand,

'Prince Henry is dead,' he announces. 'Of the typhus, they think. Though no idea how he was infected, he is so well guarded. They're scrieving sonnets to him already. They were going to be for his wedding.'

'The sum of all men's hopes ... our brave and martial prince ... which has the noble conscience ... an angel singing what you were ...'

It is a cataclysm, an apocalypse. Rachel starts weeping.

Alison finally goes into labour, an abrupt and speedy labour, she is bearing down and twisting on her bed. Rachel collects herself and goes to boil water. George rushes out to find the midwife. Alone in distress, Alison is surprised by the pain. She gives herself up and lies there, a victim to the pangs, not conquering them with a helping hand. She gasps for breath, panicking; she screams, both frail and frightened, collapses in a heap on the blankets losing consciousness.

George and Rachel try for an eternity of minutes to save her, the doctor is delayed because the streets outside throng with shocked crowds trying to verify Prince Henry's death.

But Alison cannot breathe, and George is helpless as his young wife suffocates in his arms.

Nineteen

The relentless march

James cannot conceal his fury at the relentless march of time, and the relentless march of death. These look without care on king and commoner alike. The frightening part is that all keep getting older. A poetic tribute exactly reflecting his thoughts is provided by the good Ben Jonson. It ends with a hint at hubris;

'Farewell, thou child of my right hand and joy;

My sin was too much hope of thee, loved boy.'

Powerful as he is, the King cannot control the clammy hand of mortality, which points with arbitrary finger at whomsoever it chooses.

The King's Archbishop, a Calvinist advisor, talks with glee it seems about the triumph of death and the powerlessness of the kings of this world in the face of God, who alone has power.

A realisation of his own frailty is not normal for James.

His Fool is the only one capable of giving respite:

'If cherries didn't exist, could you invent them? Probably not.'

The King's jeweller is as pale and stunned as his royal master. There is still the business of a royal wedding and when asked to make the young Princess Elizabeth's headdress for her gown, Heriot is told she will be dressed in black mourning and needs a huge brooch of jet. Black mourning for her wedding, and she a Princess! Heriot remembers the white feathers he found lying on the road during his own grief for his first wife, the delicacy of the puff of hope that keeps us alive. Tiny fragile plumes are the only headdress Elizabeth wears as she walks up the aisle aged seventeen to marry Frederick, Elector Palatine: a sound Protestant Prince.

The fashion is taken up the next day by all the young gallants at court in the city, making white feathers suddenly very expensive.

Even this marriage nearly does not take place such is the effect of the death of Prince Henry; the mourning and sorrow of the King and Queen mean they cannot bear to hold audience with anyone; the affairs of state stop. The

Palatines think they ought to leave the royal court of England to its grief and return all the way to Heidelberg. Only Lord Cecil manages to persuade the King to ask the Palatines to stay.

'There must be some joy amid all this woe. I beg your Majesty not to let the sorrow of your loss cloud your judgment or blind you to the happiness of your daughter. Should her life be blighted, saddened too? Not only is this match of good politick but the young persons are in love,' Cecil advises.

James calls for the marriage of the two seventeen-year-olds to be held on St Valentine's Day. The couple giggle helplessly at the French of Sir Thomas Lake who translates directly from the Book of Common Prayer, and whose French is very bad. The Archbishop of Canterbury has to step in and call it back to order. Many observe that the boy Frederick is much too young and puny to be a groom. However James having called them 'young turtles to be coupled on St Valentines Day,' goes to visit the morning after the wedding night to cross-examine young Frederick and make sure that the marriage has been consummated.

Elizabeth still wears black, but the feastings and celebrations are lavish. There are Masques and dancing, revels, banquets, tilting and torchlight processions. There is a mock battle acted out between boats on the Thames of a Christian navy fighting a Turkish one, with decorative costumes, costing 6000 pounds and causing the loss of three hands and two eyes among the young men who take part.

At last, as James bids farewell to his daughter and son-in-law, 'Frederick you must swear that Elizabeth your wife shall come first, take precedence at court over yourself, your mother and all other German princes because,' he emphasizes, 'she is of higher rank by birth, being daughter of a king.'

Obediently Elizabeth writes to him while waiting to sail from Margate, 'I shall perhaps never see again the flower of princes, the king of fathers, the best and most amiable father that the sun will ever see.'

The journey to Heidelberg is long and enjoyable, stopping off to visit many nobles over whom Elizabeth also takes precedence. Her French is fluent, her German improving, and she is young.

A year after losing his son, King James gains a grandchild.

Twenty

Shakespeare is leaving

James has called his court playwright, whose position he created 'for life', and expounds his own eternal situation,

'I am an only child. A precious jewel set in a golden monarchy.'

'And I am the eldest surviving of eight children, your Majestie. There are more where I come from, but you are unique.'

'Son of a glover, I hear. I never wear gloves.'

'Gloves sell in pairs.'

'Tho' some have only one hand.'

'As usual your wit is ahead of me, sire.'

'But we are not here to discuss gloves. You are leaving us.'

'Yes, sire. I leave a good company that will serve you well. The Kings Men will act my plays faithfully. Almost half are written down and the rest they know by heart. Other playwrights will jostle for my place. You will not be left without entertainment.'

'Will you not make one last theatrical, which will examine the recent past? The subject of the late Queen's father, Henry the Eighth, and his marriage to Anne Bullen. We need an example of unhappiness to show how good a king we have who is faithful to his wife.'

'And Buckingham?' Shakespeare knows that he has gone too far, to imply that the King has a lover in Lord Buckingham. He hastily covers himself. 'I will put my Lord Buckingham in the play, he shall have a part as himself.'

'Yes, why not, it is make-believe after all. And he shall have a costume all-bejewelled as he does today. And what character will you give him?'

'A good and faithful servant of the King. Gracious, kind and forgiving.'

'But does he die?'

'I don't know yet, tis not yet written, but if he dies, 'tis with honour.'

'Come into the garden.'

The garden at Theobalds, formerly the pride of Lord Cecil who gave it to the King, has been taken over by James now that the Lord has moved on; but the staff remain, and the gardeners keep the same state of perfection. A waft of roses from a bed with rosiers, ten foot high, pink and red, orange and yellow, white and light tinted rose, tended as a nursemaid would a baby, weeded and nurtured with horse dung, dug well in. The eye flies to a bank of purple lavender alive with the hum of bumblebees and the flit of white butterflies. Shakespeare stares in amazement. In a fine lace ruff and a finely edged beard, he has an almost childlike face, with the most sensitive eyes James has ever seen. He looks as though he is seeing things for the very first time, the way an infant does.

'Their wing marks are drawn so fine, as if with charcoal.'

He says of the Cabbage Whites and instantly regrets his artlessness as the King asks his gloved attendant to catch a butterfly to see for sure.

White kid gloves are not subtle enough to safely catch an insect and all that is left for the King to examine is a wing. But he verifies and admires the pencil grey markings on the inner wing.

'So delicate, like one of your sonnets.'

'You have read my sonnets?'

'No, but I am told they are fine.'

Shakespeare sees that if the King likes or needs him, he will not get away, he will never return home to his wife and modest house and garden. He will remain like a butterfly caught with a clumsy glove.

'No, your Majestie, the sonnets are not good. The plays are ephemera. They are all nothing compared to this garden.'

The yews are cut in great perfect balls, not a twig out of place, like a lady's wig. The paths are edged with sculpted grey stones, granite perhaps, sparkling when the sun catches them. There are chairs with embroidered cushions in the same carved stone, and cherry trees dotted around with ripe, red offerings. The King asks his white-gloved attendant to pass him a few juicy fruits and offers two to Shakespeare.

'Thank you, you have created a splendid park. May you always have the good health to enjoy it.'

He is now desperate to escape. 'May I take these to my …' he is just about to say wife, but possibly the King knows she is far away in Stratford, 'My cast?'

'Your cast?'

'My players, my friends?'

'Yes,' the King knows he wants to go, and waves him away as his Lord Buckingham approaches. 'What are you doing, my Lord?

'Nothing 'I wasted time, and now time doth waste me.' Replies Buckingham swiftly

'A pretty line.'

'One of his, your Majesty.' He indicates the retreating Shakespeare, who is silently composing the next play, and in turn a line appears in his mind as he turns to look at Buckingham:

'Ye have angels' faces, but heaven knows your hearts.'

Twenty-One

Libellule – Dragonfly

Heriot now has no one, no wife, no child, let alone a grandchild, although he is the age of the King and, some whisper, is richer than the King, because the King of course has debts, and Heriot only has debtors.

With all his money he is desolate. Better to be a spendthrift, to distribute cheerfully like the King. But this is not his nature, and he knows he is a canny Scot and James is simply a king.

Rachel is always watching, reflecting as he comes home each evening. She is not grey yet, still brown-haired and bonnie, kind-faced, not really beautiful, but nice. No point in falling in love again, just take what is offered and she is sympathetic. She knows him, perhaps she loves him.

Rachel is a mainstay. She offers comfort and, though advanced in years, becomes pregnant. But he cannot marry his housekeeper; not wishing to tempt fate, he can never marry again. The child survives. He is more than pleased, keeping them both at home, and promises Rachel that at his demise he will entail the house here in St Martin in the Fields to his daughter Liza. Her surname is Band, like Rachel.

A peace descends upon his household. Rachel, though not his wife, has the place of one and employs more staff. She has her own bedchamber with her daughter and does not encumber her master with demands as a wife would. Though she is there. George does not wish to have another child, so after some time he ceases to visit her room.

Rachel has made their small garden a place of roses and lavender, sage, parsley and rosemary. It smells sweet to sit in and she brings him drinks that he sips like the insects, which sip nectar from flowers. There is a small pond with lilies and frogs; over them spin blue dragonflies.

One July morning at 11 o' clock, in the strong morning sunshine, he is sitting in the garden with his ledgers, when a turquoise dragonfly flies straight into his mouth. Before he has time to know what has happened, he swallows the prickly insect and coughs, amazed. Liza who is five years old, points and says seriously, 'Libellule, Lee-be-lool. Dragonfly.'

George does not know what is more astonishing, the fly in his mouth or his child speaking French. Even the mere existence of his daughter is to be thankful – every moment is precious. He has come a long way since the days in Fishmarket Close, with the waft of fish guts on a warm morning. He has witnessed a pageant of governance, of kingship and queenship. It is on this day, twenty-five years ago, that he was appointed by James, then the sixth of Scotland, as goldsmith to his Queen. His children have died, but so have many of hers. Out of seven births, his Queen has two live children.

George rarely sees Anna now. There are numerous court jewellers, though he is still the favourite, and still the first person the Queen calls when she needs money.

His weight glues him to his chair. Twenty years ago he would have leapt up, spat out the insect and ran for a glass of water. But thoughts are heavy things, and his daughter is a marvel. He swallows again and says jokingly,

'Mmm, c'etait bon.'

Liza laughs, she does not believe him, but sits down beside the pond examining the lilies and water beetles.

Glued to his chair is just where he must be. There are one hundred and fifty-three lines of figures to finish in his book-keeping. His passion and dedication to his account books has never wavered in all the years at court. He has never engaged another junior keeper of accounts. Life may vary, but numbers never do; they have a security like no other.

'You will burn sitting here in the sun.' Says a voice at his shoulder. It is Rachel.

'It couldn't be a pleasanter burning,' he assures her. He takes her hand and together they look at the living child, whose wonder at insects thrills them through.

'Papa ate a libelule,' she calls from the pond.

'Come inside, both of you. You will burn in the sun.'

As ever, it is the attention to the small detail in life that brings them through. Liza has survived by minute management, every cough and sigh is interpreted and action accorded. George gets the same attention, if not more, as he is still her master, and Rachel does not ask for a higher station.

They have a cat now, which approaches with bristling, avuncular whiskers and seeds in his coat. George removes the seeds and the cat, at the implied invitation, jumps on his lap then his books, knocking into his inkwell.

Liza picks up her pet, 'Jimmy, Jimmy, Jimmy.'

'You named him after your king.'

'Is that treason?'

'Not in my house.'

'He might live longer. Does a cat live longer than a king?'

George leans back in his chair, feeling the sun warmed wood against his body and, not wishing to make her fear the death of her cat, replies,

'It depends on the king.'

Twenty-Two

Ben Jonson walks to Scotland

'But Scotland, your Majesty, must I go there? They cannot read or write and there is nothing but bloodshed and witchcraft.'

'The visit will cure your ignorance! And I insist that you walk there, so you can talk to those Scots you fear so much. You will stay with William Drummond of Hawthornden Castle, near Edinburgh, who is a poet like yourself.'

'Aye, his "Tears on the Death of Moeliades" is a tribute worthy of Prince Henry, God rest his soul.'

'He is a nephew of my Gentleman Usher, and a friend of Heriot my jeweller. He will welcome you like a lost brother.'

'I met him near ten years ago on the occasion of the visit of King Christian of Denmark, your beloved brother-in-law. He penned some verses then, but was being sent to France to learn the Law.'

'He is a good, learned, Protestant soul and a nobleman.'

'Tis true, I am not noble by birth, but I am noble by choice. Although it is not my choice to be a little lame.'

'Nonetheless you will walk there, to cure your lameness and your ignorance.'

Jonson, a writer by trade and not in his first youth, at nearly fifty and weighing almost twenty stone, is not the fittest candidate for a four-hundred-mile walk. However he is not lacking in courage and walk he does. It is wet and cold that autumn, but being a King's Emissary, he is entertained at noble houses all the way along the road north. He does not walk more than ten miles a day and takes Sundays off.

His reluctance to reach the colder climes makes dallying more pleasant. Bobbing manes clop past with an enviable rhythm; they have four legs and Ben has two; in particular a grey ridden by a young boy glide alongside and the horse eyes him in the patient and knowing way of animals. It is in all a humbling experience. It takes ten weeks to walk with his staff and his ready wit. But he is buoyed-up by those he meets, his spirits climb as he crosses the border and the friendliness of the folk on his route surprises him, warming his heart. He regrets his belief, and that of most of the Court in London, that the Scots as a race are nasty, brutal and ignorant. Some are as learned as he, and many are more sophisticated, even among the ladies. He even discovers that he has Scots ancestors, half of whom were women.

At last he reaches the gatehouse of Hawthornden with its pine needle path through an avenue of yew to the ancient fortress. A red sandstone keep, with narrow slit windows, guards a pleasant courtyard, which sits atop a cliff falling into a ravine with a river in spate below. The master himself comes out to greet him, saying, in metre,

'Welcome, welcome, royal Ben.'

And Jonson cannot resist finishing the couplet, 'Thank ye, thank ye, Hawthornden.'

That sets the tone for their stay. Each night William Drummond keeps a diary of the conversations with Ben, who regales him with the news of Court, the best poets, who is in and who is out, who is dead and who alive, how Heriot's second wife is dead but he has a child by his housekeeper, but marry again he will not in case it jinx the child.

'Heriot's a God-fearing man, not superstitious at all,' protests Hawthornden.

'But lost too many bairns as you say here, too many dead bairns, and he mourns their loss and talks of how they would be educated and how they would inherit his fortune, but none live. So he will not marry her, and hopes their child will live,' explains Jonson with passion.

Both writers wear white lace ruffs to frame the face, the more delicate the lace the finer the frame, and of course, it marks the gentlefolks out from servants.

Drummond is an aristocratic laird, learned and polite, speaking Latin, Greek, Italian, French and Spanish. Jonson is a self-made man, a successful playwright, with experience in bricklaying and soldiering, has a cockney accent and belief in himself that pushes the bubble of self-importance well before anyone else. They make for good company. In fact, Drummond discovers, Jonson was educated at Westminster School, the very best, before his descent into bricklaying, and as a soldier he has killed a man close up in a knife battle.

'A great lover and praiser of himself, a condemner and scorner of others,' Drummond notes in his diary.

By this point Drummond is not best pleased that Jonson considers himself so superior. In his library, he shows Jonson that he has read books as follows:

'Two hundred and sixty-seven in Latin

Thirty-five in Greek

Eleven in Hebrew

Eight in Spanish

Sixty-one in Italian

One hundred and twenty in French, and only fifty in English.'

'Why only fifty in English?' asks the patriot Jonson, who is in high animal spirits every evening. Offended by this pro-European slight, he offers a criticism in return.

'You are too good and simple, Drummond, and often a man's modestie makes a fool of his wit.'

'I know no other way,'

'Ye know little. Yet you do know of Southwell – Thomas Southwell, the Jesuit. The man was hanged for his beliefs, a Catholic, and I myself was of that sympathy but would not die for it. Yet if I had written his short poem the 'Burning Babe', I would have been content to destroy all of my long works.

"The fuel Justice layeth on, and Mercy blows the coals,

The metal in this furnace wrought are men's defiled souls"

So simple and clean. I was in a prison like he, and inquisitioned on my religion, but I am not one to die for my faith. He did.'

'Were you there also for your conscience?'

'No, I killed a man.'

'Another?'

'For a soldier, a killing is not alien. We think it through, practice it, make it sport, then it becomes easy. Just as a bedding is easy for a whore. Yet when we do it, we are imprisoned.'

'And rightly so. There is a difference between killing in battle and killing in the streets.'

'In the streets you see the old soldiers, with a sign that says, "I was taught to kill men, not to grow food. Please strangers, have mercy on your defenders." For we are your defenders, you meek and mild walkers of the town. You goodly men and women who abhor bloodshed.'

'I will remember that the next time I pass an old soldier beggar. In case he kills me.'

'All vice springs from ignorance.'

'I thank you for dispelling my own. I always thought ingratitude the worst vice.'

'Yes, we must be grateful to our soldiers. But we digress. I was imprisoned for murder, not for matters of conscience like Thomas Southwell ...'

It seems that Jonson is a good man in fact and cannot put behind him his forced public disavowal of his faith.

'My sympathy', he explains, 'is not for fracturing our religions in two, and punishing one, and championing the other, but for each man to have freedom in his choice of belief and for each to live alongside the other in harmony.'

They have much conversation on this subject of Catholics and Protesters, and Calvinists and Covenanters and ask, as each professes to love Jesus Christ, then why do they kill each other?

Drummond also likes to hear the gossip from Court and Jonson is merry with his tales.

He says, 'Queen Elizabeth could not be wed because she had a thick membrane that could not be pierced in her maiden part ...'

'How do you know that?' interrupts William.

'From her doctor, of course. Who else?'

Living at Court he hears all the tales of a poisoner who was the best dressmaker. And of Thomas Overbury who was killed it seems because he did not consummate his marriage. He continues, 'Except that his wife was a young maid in love with the King's favourite, and so had to be wed to him.'

'The King wanted his favourite wed?' asks Hawthornden.

'Of course, so as not to seem his favourite, though gifts lavished on him cost more than a new cathedral.'

'The waste, the waste,' moans his host, 'when you think on those that starve for a few pennies.'

Walks in the grounds of Hawthornden Castle are slippery in the frost. Why choose winter to visit Scotland? He cannot answer for his King. The castle is perched on a cliff and looking out gives him vertigo.

The iron latch on the studded oak door creaks and aches as he leaves for the vast unkempt and dangerous grounds, the precipice, the unguarded well and overhanging rock – where William goes to contemplate The Fall of Man. Water cascading down below reminds him of his own mortality. And this is all his host likes to think on, notes Jonson with humour, picking his way among the frozen leaves beneath the skeletal trees in the last light of afternoon. The reason being that William's great love, Mary, died on her wedding night three years ago. Since then he has not looked on another woman. The solitude and warmth of his small bedroom with its fire calms him, along with the fellowship of meals:

'Go to, young William! Liven yourself up. Think of posterity if not of your own health. 'Tis not good for a man of your age to self-inflict the pain of solitude, for you to have an empty bed when there are plenty fertile maids around. Think of them, their future, their benefit. You can feed another mouth! And if not that, then what about your lands? Who will inherit this castle? Fill it full of children, man. Unbutton yourself.'

Jonson has a soldiersome way with words, which does not incline the refined Drummond to do any such thing. He is still working on sonnets in praise of the perfection of his angelic but now dead wife.

'Did you never kiss her?' asks Jonson.

'If I did I would not speak of it.'

'My own wife is old,' confides Jonson, 'We know each other too well. She is a shrew, yet honest.'

'I don't like women of character myself,' adds William. 'Forcefulness should be left to men.'

'I agree,' nods his guest.

At that point the cook enters to let them know, with great force, that supper is waiting, and could they please bring through their own glasses and sit at the table before it gets cold. Both men jump in obedience as if drilled and walk through to the dining room without questioning her authority.

Twenty-Three
The fuel of justice

'Guid sheep heid stew,' announces the tough-looking cook, proud to provide a local staple for the English visitor.

Jonson is taken aback at the whole sheep's head on his plate, surrounded by a clutch of vegetables and a thick brown gravy. He is about to protest that he cannot attempt such a mountain of food, when there is a loud banging at the door.

Then a shouting and high-pitched wailing and a scuffle.

Drummond excuses himself, but Jonson follows through to the small, stone-flagged entry hall with its fire and tapestry over the door. Douglas, his aging manservant, has just thrown out, 'a beggar wumman'.

Drummond opens the huge oak door to find the creature sitting on the frozen step in the wet, her ragged shawl clutched around her head, and in her arms a small parcel.

She stands at once and begs,

'Maister Drummond, hear me, I beg ye.'

Drummond shows her in and sees to his surprise that the small parcel is about two years old, with hollow eyes and a blue complexion.

'They've ta'en ma guidman, as good and honest as ye are yersel. I ask ye, maister, tae find him and I can prove that he did not kill yon deer. It wis already deid.'

Douglas wants to show her out again.

'The poacher, her man's the poacher you turned over last week.'

'I am entertaining my friend to dinner.'

'No, please, I am delighted.' Jonson is ushering the woman and child into the dining room and giving them chairs. 'Please, Drummond, I cannot eat a whole sheep's head.'

He pushes his plate towards the woman and child.

The child and his mother fall on the food as if starving, which they likely are.

In between mouthfuls, 'Normally ye wouldna eat a deid hind. But in the snaw, it canny go aff, and if ye tak oot the liver…ken whit a mean? Ken whit a mean? Ken whit a mean?'

Jonson weighs in, 'Yes, you mean the deer was already dead. It's not poaching, Drummond. Can we find this poor man?'

'Aye, he wis takin' oot the liver by the burn, when the factor spied him. And that was it. Nae questions asked. He's clappit in irons and is aff awa' tae the jile.'

'And now there is no one to provide for his wife and child, but you, Drummond. A miscarriage of justice is expensive.'

'If it is a miscarriage, how can anyone prove the deer was already dead?'

'You have their word for it.' He indicates the hollow-eyed two-year-old, who nods emphatically along with his mother, who cannot be more than eighteen herself.

Although she is cramming her dirty face with food, clutching a wet shawl, and gabbling fast about her man, there is a savage beauty about her that the men cannot help noticing. It is lucky.

Jonson, ever alert to attraction, offers her a glass of wine, which she refuses, seeing Drummond's disapproving eye.

'Can I dry ma shawl?' she asks.

Jonson takes it and spreads it on the back of a chair in front of the fire.

She is wearing a torn dress, also wet.

'Come and sit near the heat. What is your name?'

'Mary'.

Drummond winces. He does not like to think of another Mary, one that is not his own sweetheart, sanctified and pure.

This Mary, here before him, no doubt unmarried but with a child, and a man, so she says, in prison, so she must be strong, but is not yet twenty, and has no food. Where does she live? How does she live? He can help her for the sake of his dead Mary. Meanwhile he notices Jonson who is moving closer to the girl and being gallant, something Mary has no experience of, she does not know how to respond. Drummond turns her attention to her child.

'What's the name of your bairn, Mary?'

'Johnnie. He's gey wee fur twa. But he's strang.'

Johnnie nods again, vigorously, cramming mashed turnips into his mouth.

She avoids Jonson, and looks to Drummond, 'I'd be gratefu' if ye'd find his faither, maister. And see him released fae the jail.'

'I will see what I can do, Mary.'

'Let's pen the letter now,' offers Jonson, a little precipitously.

'We have drunk but we have not eaten,' says Drummond. 'The letter we can do tomorrow.'

'The morn's too late,' says Mary.

'Yes, tomorrow's too late. Do it now.' Jonson is excited by the woman, the wine, the miscarriage of justice, and the chance to pen a letter. 'I'll do it. I can take my wine. I am in full possession of my faculties. The lovely Mary is in distress, and her child is hungry. Let's not delay.'

Mary allows Jonson to move closer to her. He puts his hand on her shoulder, then goes up the stairs to the study to fetch pen and paper. Drummond sees a situation going well beyond his control and Douglas, watching and hearing all, does not approve.

'Ye can gie me a letter, maister, but none will read it till the morn anyway. And the night is in, the path slipperie, I'll not deliver tonight,' says his canny, faithful servant. 'Ye may as well see the wumman out and gie her some bread for the morn.'

But Jonson reappears with paper, ink and pen and places them on the dining tablecloth with a flourish.

'Wait, let's clear the dinner,' suggests Drummond.

Douglas shifts uneasily as the cook takes the empty plates from the uninvited guests, then leaves the room in distaste.

But nothing hinders Jonson. He blithely begins the letter, 'What is the name of your magistrate? Is he your friend, Drummond?'

'My dear Jonson, we shall not do this now,' says the gentle host.

'Perhaps a man's life hangs on it.'

'Then allow this young lady to leave.'

'She is still wet. And so beautiful.'

Mary blushes, knowing it all to be improper, but desperate to get her man free, is prepared to do anything for that. Drummond fears the situation getting ever more out of hand.

Douglas enters with a helpful suggestion. 'Let Mary and the bairn dry themselves in the kitchen. The fire's bigger and there's mair food.'

Thankful, Drummond swiftly ushers them out, saying,

'Now, my good and merciful friend. We will write the letter. The sheriff is my brother-in-law.'

Remembering that he has forgotten himself, Jonson reconciles himself to the loss of a woman, but the gaining of a letter. The men work for a good ten minutes on a short missive which will ensure the release of the poacher caught with the deer at Hawthornden last week.

The cook enters. 'Wae's me, the sheep heid's a' eaten.'

Relieved, Jonson says, 'But justice is done, good woman. Bread and cheese and wine must suffice for our stomachs.'

Twenty-Four
Aztec Gold

A satisfying clop and clatter on the road south marks
Jonson's triumphant return, this time by horse, to London.
The clang of church bells sounds from the villages through
the fields calling the people to prayer or to service or to
whatever form of worship is now permitted, as the country
turns from one Christian religion to the next in obedience
to the dictats of the latest classification of faith. The heavy
haze of harvest hangs above the bent backs of the men in
the meadows. The wheat is dry and bristles like a golden
brush, ready for the lines of wielded sickles. Women work
alongside, fetching pitch-forks and rakes, bringing food and
tools, carrying baskets and creels wearing long skirts, with
sunburnt arms and white hats. Two yellow insects on top
of each other fly before him and he realizes, enviously, that

dragonflies copulate while air borne. He checks an impulse to slide off his horse and walk through the haystacks.

Mesmerised by other people at work, Jonson is enthralled by the scenes before him. A breath of warm wind blows across the light bronze fields, the wheat stems shine as they fall, and the sound of the tolling bells rolls over the stubble.

Bells are always tolling for someone, and the news when Jonson arrives in London is not so idyllic.

Jonson's friend Sir Walter Raleigh has been executed by royal order; and all because of Spain. So he is given to understand through the lengthy machinations of his tired King who now knows that whatever he decides, someone will get the chop.

Raleigh, national hero and explorer of the New World, was already in the Tower for thirteen years before he was finally allowed out again to lead a naval force to Orinoco to stake a British claim to what Spain sees as their own conquered lands.

'He set sail across the ocean again?' Jonson asks of his friends,

'Raleigh cannot conquer Orinoco from the Tower, so let him out why not?'

'Why is he there in the first place? And who is Orinoco anyway? I mean where is it?' Jonson needs all the detail.

'The Indies.'

A murmuring Lord beside him tries to explain. 'He is seen as the enemy of Spain for his rigorous Protestant views. But his grandfather was tortured by bloody Mary so the ancestral pride in what he died for is under strain.'

Jonson too is weary of this religious struggle: this constant bicker over whose path to God is correct and whose is not and therefore heresy: decapitation of someone is always the result.

'So Spain insisted Raleigh be killed?' asks Jonson. 'And all for Orinoco?'

'Raleigh did not do the deed.'

'No, his name was Kismet,'

'Not Kismet (that is fate) but Keymis ...'

'Yes, his follower and loyal friend, who fired on and burnt the Spanish town of St Thomas in Guiana, and in the process Raleigh's son was killed by a musket bullet in one go.'

'Poor, poor man. His son was killed before him?' Jonson sags in sadness.

'King James was so annoyed at the Spanish ambassador who asked that Raleigh be hanged in Madrid, that he threw his hat on the floor.'

'Our good King threw his hat on the floor? That is something. Did it still have its jewel?'

'I was there. It clattered against the stone steps like a wee crown itself, and Cecil picked it up, the creep.'

'So Raleigh is thrown back in the tower again – where he had been languishing we know for thirteen long years

before under a death penalty, for treason, but being liked
and the King compassionate he is still alive.'

'Not now.'

'They say he burnt a whole Spanish town.'

'They are angry.'

'Incandescent. Spanish fury.'

'Raleigh had to be tried again. And this time the deed
was done.'

'He did agree to go to the scaffold. Many friends tried
to let him escape, but die he would, little heart had he left,
after the death of his son.'

'He was not shaking out of fear on the scaffold but from
an illness he got in Orinoco. He needed medicine and said
of the axe, asking to feel it, "This is a sharp medicine, but
it's a physician for all diseases and miseries."'

"Strike man, strike!" were his last words to the
executioner.'

Jonson does not wholly understand his King's relations
with the Spanish and the New World. Raleigh had told
the King that there was gold, mines of gold, and that
these were not Spanish but belonged to the natives. Also
he claimed that the whole area of Guiana was claimed for
England, and he had staked that claim before he was ever
put in the tower. But during these thirteen years of Raleigh
in prison in The Tower of London, the Spanish got on with
their conquering. They took their orders from the Pope, a
superior authority, and the Pope had signed a document

giving Spain the world authority to convert the savages. In the process of this conversion to the Catholic faith, with the help of Jesuits and Franciscan missionaries, much gold had been taken from the locals. Raleigh believed that it should be English gold. He said he staked his claim to this land long before he was imprisoned and his imprisonment has meant that England has missed out on conquering the New World.

'And its the King's Catholic sympathy that lost us New World gold!'

'A mistake.'

'Well now Raleigh is dead.'

'God rest his soul.'

He was ever brilliant but unstable. A poet, a writer, a husband to only one woman, and much of his life lived out not in the wide stretches of the ocean but in a cramped prison room.

Jonson hears of this piece by piece from various friends at Court and friends in the tavern. The latter are furious, Raleigh was a hero, and it is this new King's soft approach to Catholic Europe that is at fault. We English need separation and independence, none of your wet alliances with Spain. A cry of 'No Popery' goes up from the small table of rowdy drinkers.

'It's said that the King seeks to marry his son to a Spanish Princess, a Catholic.'

England has never liked Europe.

'We do not need them. We can fight the world alone.'

The smell of the tavern is of sweat, of beer, of pickles, and Jonson feels nauseous. The small concerns of his quiet walking trip to Scotland and the calm of the landscape are far behind him now. What sickens him most is the unnecessary waste of life of a man so brilliant with such knowledge and wisdom, courage and leadership. James has cut off a man of sixty-five years, who has so many admirers and followers, and all to appease Spain, which country we were lately at war with. It does not make sense. But as any playwright knows, politics never makes sense, it is the job of the writer to order events and present them as sense.

Twenty-Five

Bohemian rupture

George Heriot in his small, happy world cannot shut out the news from Court, which is often about great violence committed on a soul. He can no longer bear to hear the details of torture, or death by hanging, or execution by axe. Yet it is news lapped-up by many; it is surprising the level of character that likes the talk of destruction.

If a man can deliver and discuss it without a flinch he is described as manly, and if he avoids it, he is womanly. George is seen as womanly, but then all the artisans of court are womanly, especially those who pen sonnets. Ladies of the court on the other hand must wince when they over-hear death gossip – for they do not wish to be seen as unwomanly. Lady Marjorie is good at wincing, though it is unconvincing.

A new agitation visits the court – one that permits both men and women to flinch lightly and even chuckle deeply. In Bohemia, two Protestant nobles break into the Palace in Prague and throw two Catholic nobles out of the window. King James hears of the event with a certain glee and allows the Bohemian ambassador an immediate audience.

'His excellency Luka von Modrich, ambassador of Bohemia.'

A slim, boyish figure enters, his long hair flipping over his eyes and a strange leather headband holding straggling bits of lank fringe from obscuring his view.

James utters loudly, 'Who has sent a child to me? Is this emissiary twelve years old?'

Von Modrich has a distant, poetic look in his slanting eyes and, expressionless, he replies to the King. 'I am thirty-two, your Majesty. I rode here, hence a certain fatigue.'

'You rode from Bohemia? Some horseman is that. Give the man food.'

'Your Highness,' he continues, breathless but upright, 'I am here to bid you support the Protestant nobles of Bohemia.'

'Against the Catholics – you know I will not do that. That way war lies. I will not start another Reformation. I will help you make peace. Bohemia is Hapsburg and backed by Spain, our ally. But first eat, man, you are too serious. Give him wine.'

All eyes turn to the slight but powerful figure, noticing his strong, cross-gartered legs and dark green velvet breeches, worn but thick. On top is a doublet of the same velvet and over all a dense woollen cloak, fringed with an unknown fur.

He has an exotic attraction: silent, straight, self-possessed.

As the days pass and the story unfolds it transpires that von Modrich excels not so much at diplomacy, but at sport. His swordsmanship is wholly fascinating; his riding skilled. The King takes him hunting, just to watch him on a horse, which he rides with a speed that outruns the deer, standing in the stirrups with the same distant expression he has when standing still at court.

He persists in his request for support, not financial, just a letter, an official declaration of support to the Protestant faction in Bohemia.

But James does not want to interfere, he is the Rex Pacificus, the Peaceful King, and his second-best playwright pens a pamphlet to be distributed to the people at large declaring that he is so. 'Here sits Solomon and hither come his tribes for judgement'. The Spanish ambassador, more vocal than the Bohemian, secretly reports, 'The vanity of the present king of England is so great, that any peace obtained must issue from him alone. He knows that if he wants a Spanish bride for his last remaining son, he cannot support usurpers in Bohemia.'

Luca von Modrich is unmoved, and persistent. The King does not want him to leave because the Bohemian's riding and swordplay are too entertaining. Von Modrich even plays with the servant children who are kicking a pig's bladder round the kitchen yard. He flicks the bladder into the air with a deft hook of his foot and keeps it up with knee and ankle and heel in front, behind and sideways. His skill enthralls the children, the servants and the courtiers, who hang out of the windows to watch. He becomes a favourite, always with his leather headband, which has a small, carved stone at the fore. One of the children has the temerity to point it out and he straightens instantly and stops playing.

None of the adults ask him about his head decoration, and no lady succeeds in getting close enough to question. He is distant with the court ladies, no matter how coquettish they are with him. Perhaps they bore him. Still he does not leave.

After a successful hunt one day, where he rides superbly but never shoots, von Modrich has the place of honour beside the King for dinner. The plush of his green velvet doublet is faded from days spent outside in the saddle, his hair seems unwashed though still kept in place by the mysterious headband, but his expression is unaltered since the first day. He addresses the King, only after being asked to, and one day replies,

'The throne of Bohemia must pass to a good Protestant Prince, of which there are few – Frederick, Elector Palatine, comes to mind.'

'But that is a different idea,' announces the King, 'and a good one. Frederick is married to my daughter, Elizabeth, you are no doubt aware. She would make a good Queen – maybe even a great Queen. She is of course the daughter of a Queen.'

'And you would be father-in-law to the King of Bohemia,' suggests the Bohemian at once, 'We would all owe you allegiance. I cannot think of a more worthy allegiance.'

This is the first time von Modrich has stooped to flattery, and his head inclines slightly.

The King understands the concession, he proposes a toast:

'Here's to von Modrich, a man who has changed the fortunes of his country simply by being a good sport.'

There is clapping and cheers all round from the Court, who have no idea where Bohemia is but do know that this is a good rider and swordsman. Few can suspect the machinations inside the tortured King's head. Gondomar, Spanish ambassador, sits to his left, and now rises to leave the hall and set sail at once for Spain in a fury.

Spain does not need a Protestant king inside what they see as the Holy Roman Empire. If King James does in fact want to be the progenitor of World Peace and marry his son to the Infanta of Spain, then he cannot support as King and Queen of Bohemia members of his own Protestant family. James is equally moved by Gondomar. Of course he wishes, like God, to bring peace unto the world, and to be known for it. He wants to be on good terms with everyone, with Gondomar, with von Modrich, with his family at home and with his Palatine daughter and son-in-law.

It would be so much easier to be a good king if everyone loved him and he loved everyone.

Just as he allows himself to feel that warm wine of human compassion, as befits his age, experience and wisdom, another death comes crashing into the monarch's life.

Twenty-Six

Death of Queen Anna

'If you lace a woman that tight, she's bound to swell up and burst like a pig's bladder.'

'She did die of swelling. That is the cause of death.'

'And nine times she was with child. Each time she was laced up so that she looked slim as a young girl. No wonder so few of her children survived.'

'And how old was she?'

'Forty-five. Not old, still good for child-bearing.'

Rachel's friends are gathering over the garden gate by the Heriot household, one carrying washing in a basket, and another eggs.

Rachel herself bore Liza at forty-five. She is lucky, so lucky that never a day passes without her being thankful. Now sorrow at the death of George's patron, their

Queen, his champion, takes over. She hands the clothes for washing to one friend and takes eggs from the other as her face shows signs of trouble. They are both waiting for her reaction; at least some response from one so close, so few removes from the Queen, is meat and drink to even an amateur gossip at the washing pool. Sensing this, Rachel is silent, and, raising a hand to wave them goodbye, suggests,

'My bread will burn. I must go inside at once.'

She has avoided commenting but sitting there inside is George. He is at the round table in the hall, head down, hiding his sorrow. She approaches silently and places a strong, work-worn hand on his shoulder. He does not respond. Slowly he takes her other hand in his and holds it to his mouth, then to his eyes, where she can feel the wet of his tears.

As always when loss affects him, George embeds himself in his work, but concentration evades him this time. The woman in his life who outlived his wives, who was his Queen, his raison d'etre, his métier, his job for life, his move to London abandoning his ain country; the pearl among all others, for whom the greatest jewels in the entire world were not good enough. It is a cut loss that aches in his whole being. For nearly thirty years he has embellished her beauty with the most precious gems the earth can provide and seen the results of his labour on her person time and again. He cannot believe he will no longer see that studied enhancement of regal splendor, his life's work. For which, believing in her virtue, he was proud on a daily basis.

The King will continue to give him work, that is not in doubt, but of his virtue George is less convinced. Anna lived a life of pearl-like purity. She loved first her husband, then fought and suffered for the lives of her many children, then worked for the advancement of the arts, which benefit mankind. And to die so young, even before her own renowned and competent mother, Queen Dowager Sophie of Denmark, said to be the richest woman in northern Europe. Care of finance was not Anna's gift, however, and George accepted and supported that, being her personal banker of jewels. Now there are banks of jewels in her deceased possession and banks of debts owed to Heriot. He is a richer, if sadder man.

The King soon sends for his jeweller and gives him an important commission. A jewel he has never made before, a jewel for a headband. His King is so taken with the young Bohemian ambassador that he wants to give him a gift and upgrade the headband he wears with one that looks more expensive. It is to be leather still, that is something the man affects well, but to have a curious stone in the centre, a topaz or citrine, or a large opal that winks orange and blue when warm.

'You have met the man, Heriot. Find something that suits his fit.'

Heriot in his own heavy mood, finds something dark and purple, deep as velvet, spinel or alexandrite. He crafts the cut with care; it reflects his own many-faceted despair at the loss of three loved women in his life. Why he should cut this into a young man's jewel he does not know; but this is no ordinary young man, his eyes show a knowledge greater than his age. As George sits at his workbench cutting with his eyeglass for the first time in months, his apprentices scrutinise the work. He has not lost his touch. It is a sultry May and thunder rumbles in the sky turning the clouds a yellow black, while the streets shimmer with a light rain. George works away for hours, through the evening at the stone, oblivious to his apprentices finishing, leaving, bidding goodnight.

He has spoken with Luca von Modrich and learned he is an Utraquist Hussite, which sounds to him like the name of a gem, but is in fact a special brand of Protestant, fomenting their distaste for decades at rule by the Hapsburg Holy Roman Empire. His straight mission is to persuade the King of England to support a Protestant King in Bohemia, and Frederick, James's son-in-law, is qualified, Palatine being the highest-ranking Elector for the Holy Roman Empire. Of course, the role will be greater than simple kingship, it is a God-given task to spread the protesting faith. This is what gives von Modrich his salient purity, and that is admirable to George Heriot. His task to decorate the young Bohemian goes beyond beauty.

He hands the jewel to the King the very next day because James in turn, to distract himself, is showering attention on von Modrich. His Fool is there to present something that will lighten the King's burden and provide a show for the happening of the presentation of the jewel. The Fool arrives carrying a small theatre frame around himself with orange velvet curtains which work as he pulls a string. He mimes appearing and disappearing, takes satirical bows and claps, collapses on his knees but still manages the closing string, and has the Court in fits of laughter at his witty gestures. But he is never a Fool without a wise word, and at the end announces,

'Curtains, my lords and ladies,

We do have curtains in a day; they are morning, noon and night.'

At each he closes and opens his little theatre.

'And in a man these are birth, growth and death.'

A sigh all round.

'Curtain rise, and curtain fall, but the story goes on and nothing finishes.'

A viol plays as the Fool capers out of the hall. A trumpet sounds and the King announces,

'Luca von Modrich, for your ambassadorial panache – for hunting and the game of course, and as a fond gesture of our support of the cause of the Kingdom of Bohemia, where we do hope our daughter will be Queen, please allow me to replace that worn out circlet and present you with a jewelled one.'

Von Modrich, blushing at the attention, but instantly aware of the political significance of the gesture, strides forward on his short, powerful legs and bounds up the steps to the dais of the throne, removing his old headdress as he bows tautly before the King.

James places the circlet lovingly over his head, making von Modrich redden all the more as he genuflects before the monarch, who regards himself second only to God.

Twenty-Seven
The Hat Jewel

The world divides into two sorts of people: those who have been hurt and those who have not: the straight-forward and the apologetic; the whole and the broken.

Clarissa has a beautiful name and face. Her hair is long, light brown and shining, her hands slender and attentive to detail. She sews hats in the light of the only window in the shop and some of these lie around, carefully displayed on the small tables. They are confections of colour and lace, feathers and dried flowers, pieces of velvet and what looks like jewels but must be painted glass.

George feigns an interest in the latter. Clarissa knows who he is.

'Did Luca send you?'

There is a hint of desperation in her eyes. She rises and George can see she is with child.

'Yes,' he lies.

Von Modrich has not sent him. He is too subtle a diplomat for that. Knowing he must return to Bohemia with the news of England's support, he tells only the discreet George Heriot about his London love.

Why not take her back to Prague as his wife? He already has a betrothed, chosen for him since long ago, waiting for him. Besides Clarissa is a Catholic, a secret one but…

Luca pushes a leather purse towards George, 'Gelt'. George pushes it back: the last thing he needs is gold. But he will visit her.

'It's for her, you fool, not you. She needs care,' insists Luca with sorrow, love and pity in his face, 'but don't you go; it will frighten her. Send a woman.'

George nods.

'Farewell my good friend. I leave part of myself behind. But I serve my country first.'

George rises, 'Don't start any wars.'

The ambassador leaves for Bohemia and starts what history later calls The Thirty Years War.

It does not take long after his departure for George to launch himself through the backstreets of the city, driven by the early loss of this new companion. Any connection with the enigmatic Luca will assuage the feeling.

So, he finds Clarissa.

And now standing before him in her extreme youth, beauty, and pregnancy, she is like a vision of the Virgin Mary – untouchable, staggering. George is blinded by the light. There is no lust in his view, no eros. How can he hand over gelt?

An older woman enters, not much older, still younger than his own housekeeper, Rachel, and mother of his own child.

George stutters: 'I need to order hats. With jewels. I will provide the jewels. I will pay well.'

Thinking on his feet as usual, he seems out of place to the woman he presumes to be Clarissa's mother.

'Do you want hats or did Luca send you? Luca von Modrich?

'Yes, von Modrich, he did. He sent this purse, being recalled to Bohemia.'

George hands over the purse to the mother and she hands it to Clarissa, who takes it with limp fingers as her hands fall by her side. She turns away, tears spurting from her eyes. Her mother goes to hold her and George leaves hurriedly.

At the end of the dirty street he turns and goes back to the shop, entering with purpose,

'I do mean to order hats. Particular hats, special hats.'

He needs hats for his hat jewels, the fashion he has created, and these hats will give Clarissa and her mother a living for years. To give them urgency now he adds,

'I need them soon.'

The mother comes forward to take his order of five Speshul Hats, writing neatly in a small book in tiny letters. George is amazed she can write, till now he only knew noble women who could read or write, and is about to ask how she learnt, when she says firmly that she will see to the order but that she must now close the shop because of the fever.

Just at that moment who should come barging into the closing shop but Lady Marjorie, almost comic in her haste, 'Ah, Heriot, I thought I'd find you here.'

'Why? I have never been here before.'

Marjorie surveys the confections, 'What beautiful hats, and I need one ... I followed you, George.'

'Why?'

'It's no yours to reason why. Sin' the death of Prince Henry, 'tis Charles wha maun succeed and in my capacitee o' Lady Ward Advisor to His Royal Highness, I am charged wi' finding a princely hat, wi wallie gowdie, as a signifier o' kingship to come. This is ane Godlie task only entrustit to the best of royal makars, and you are that.'

'So you're scooting thru' the backstreets in pursuit o' me?' He cannot conceal a wry smile.

He does not believe a word she says; her need for a hat for the Prince seems extempore. She is good at extempore.

'How is your son? The yin wha sells horses?'

'In Embro still. He's scunnert wi' London.'

'Wise man. But you?'

'I'm pleasit wi the life o' Court, and I hae a use here. The Queen did confide in me and now Prince Charles trusts me as his mother's freend. And he will be King ayont.'

'Not yet, not so fast, Lady Marjorie.'

'But ye will tak my order for a jewel?'

Distrust is exhausting, but he can at least influence some good, 'If it pleasit ye to order it fae this hat shop, your Ladyship, where I hae placit my last commaunds for hats to fit my jewels.'

'Usually it's the ither way roond. A jewel for a hat, no' a hat for a jewel.' Lady Marjorie is instantly suspicious.

Here Clarissa's mother suggests, 'The hats need to be strong enough to take the jewel.'

'And the heads to wear them,' adds Clarissa, as if in a dream.

Now Lady Marjorie is even more inventive. She looks at the pregnant girl and back at the aging Heriot and makes up her mind at once. Tired, Heriot does not protest. He leaves without her, saying he must press on.

He is reminded of the typhus and places his handkerchief over his nose as he walks back through the deserted streets.

His dog welcomes him, expecting a walk, so he takes advantage of the empty town to walk as far as the woods near St James.

George stands in the wakening woods and listens. There are few horses on the track below him. His dog digs in the leaf mould at his feet, crunching and pulling on the small tree roots like a wild pig. A dog needs sustenance just like everyone else and it strikes George that that is all he can offer Clarissa, that is what he is beholden to offer. No more. No less. A living for her lifetime and that of her child. It is a lot, but he has much. Everyone will think the child is his. So much the better. But neither she nor the child are his; nothing is his but his duty.

To hold and keep this limpid, expectant day in his hand is all he can hope for. The fragility of life appears again like the ghosts of his young wives. Touch it and it dissolves, just as gold-leaf shivers in a breath. The only way of steadying is to bind it to something strong, strong and ugly like himself he sighs.

Looking down into the well of darkness over the stricken city, his mind wanders back to Edinburgh and he knows he can rely on the good people there to carry out his wishes. He has a plan for Edinburgh, a vision for how to spend his fortune.

Twenty-Eight

February 1624 – Puir faitherless bairns

When George wakes in the night, his lungs feel heavy and painful and he knows he does not have long to live. The matter of his will oppresses him. It is far easier to lie back in his warm bed dreaming and wait for the inevitable to happen, but George wants to control the future. He knows that if he leaves no will, his numerous nephews will take all; then his two daughters, fatherless bairns as they are, will be forgotten.

The thousands owed him by the King will somehow also be forgotten. The executors must be men who know the law and who know the King. They must be men of God so as to still the inevitable squabbling that comes when a rich man dies. He chooses Walter Balcanquall, thirty-eight years old, a body with a good amount of time left to him.

Walter is from Edinburgh, where he studied for the Church at the University, and then at Cambridge. He is thoroughly respected by King James, who sent Walter as a young man to be his eyes and ears at the Synod of Dort. Here he discussed the theory of Universal Atonement for sins committed in life, and therefore understands exactly what George is thinking. Moreover, he is a friend, versed in the law, a cleric and close to the Court, his neighbour, and the pastor at St Martin in the Fields, his parish church.

That is where he is to be buried, where his body will lie, but his fortune, and this is the important part, will be extracted from the King and go home to Edinburgh. The King has abandoned Scotland, but George will not. The money will build schools and ensure that the Edinburgh he left so long ago becomes a city of the best educated people in the world.

His many siblings, in-laws, nephews, nieces and servants must all be mentioned and provided for in their lifetime, but this project to educate a whole city, will last forever.

The vision to see so far ahead is exhausting; every minute detail must be listed.

February is the month when most people die, and on the 12th of that month 1624, Walter Balcanquall attends George Heriot on his deathbed.

Here the King's jeweller reiterates his vision for the future.

'The main school will be called a hospital to cure the faitherless bairns as well as teach them. They canna learn if they are sick. The building will outlast the King, his heirs, even the Union of the Crowns.'

Within his soul there is a yearning for immortality and he lacks the faith to believe it is his for the asking. He has after all, it appears anyway, two bastard children, and has failed to carry two wives with him on life's journey. Who knows what the Lord might say? Yet he has accrued a fortune through wit and charm, hard work and diplomacy, through the legitimate exercise of his God-given talents.

'Who knows what the heavenly court will decide when the eye of the needle finally beckons.' He muses.

Balcanquall at once gives his reply, both learned and soundly Protestant; 'It is not a real needle, and needles don't beckon – they sew, they wark like all o' us and George you are an honest chiel, albeit a courtier. Ye have kists full of treasure.'

'Treisur, gowd, wallie gowdies,' murmers George. 'The real wealth o' a countree is its bairns.'

'Aye man,' he is breathless, 'all my treisur will go fae the benefit o' bairns. I saw Christ's Hospital where the puir boys are brought up and schoolit so they enter university like ony rich man's son. I will build that in my ane country.'

'You have mair siller than the King himself, wha is in your debt.'

'And we are all in debt to our ane country and that, Balcanqhall, is not this England. You will build my hospital in Edinburgh.'

'A hospital?'

'Aye, the puir are ayways sick. If we take in puir boys they will be sick, so if we build a school for them, it maun also be a hospital.'

'I shall see tae it, my freend, it'll hae the King's blessing and maun be like the castle, a castle tae learning in all its splendour.'

'Splendour is no the main thing, Balcanquall. Though splendid it will be: Inigo Jones will design it like yin o his palaces. But whit is important is the character o the staff. The man at the gate. How the laundry maid behaves is mair essential. The boys, the orphans, faitherless bairns will read a psalm afore meals, then say grace, then gie thanks tae God efter the meal. Every meal, forivver. This may be my wasted, tired auld body – but that building will be my soul.'

Balcanqhall adds with gravity, 'And your legacy to Scotland will be great. In your faith, you hae fixed your houp upon the rock o history.'

George manages a quick smile, 'I can pay for the threapin o' Godlie men. Let us pray for those wha canna…'

His mind is taut as a viol string. Too many requests, ideas, thoughts and plans. George is simply grateful not to be more powerful than his status. He longs to escape into the streets where a cool breeze makes him fresh with a whiff of winter in the air. Like an animal he feels the pull of nature and longs to head for the woods, where the last leaves are falling gently and remind him again of the endless bounty of trees. Falling leaves like gold florins, non-stop.

Above all he longs to rest with no demands on his time.

The light leaves of winter's end drift past the windows and again he is reminded of the endless generosity of his Makar, his maker, the poetic genius who imagined him into being and everything else as well.

Select Bibliography

Bates, Jonathan, *Soul of the Age: the Life, Mind and World of William Shakespeare* (London, 2009)

Constable, Archibald and Balcanquall, Walter, *Memoirs of George Heriot: Jeweller to King James VI, with an historical account of the hospital founded by him at Edinburgh* (London, 1822)

Constable, David Cecil, *The Cecils of Hatfield House* (London, 1973)

*Drummond, William and MacDonald, Robert H, William Drummond of Hawthornden : poems and prose edited by Robert H. MacDonald (*Edinburgh, *1976)*

Drummond, William, *The Works of William Drummond of Hawthornden* (Edinburgh, 1711)

Drummond, William, and Ward, W.M.C, *The Poems of William Drummond of Hawthornden*, edited by W.M.C Ward (London, 1874)

Fraser, Sarah, *The Prince who Would be King* (London, 2017)

Juhala, Amy L, *The Household and Court of King James VI of Scotland 1567-1603* (phD Thesis, University of Edinburgh, 2003)

Levi, Peter, *The Life and Times of William Shakespeare* (London, 1988)

Lockhart, Brian R, *Jinglin' Geordie's Legacy* (East Linton, 2003)

Mathew, David, *James 1* (London, 1967)

Patterson, RF, *Ben Jonson's Conversations with Drummond of Hawthornden* (London,1923)

Rowse, A.I, *Shakespeare the Man* (London, 1988)

Rowse, A.I, *William Shakespeare* (London, 1995)

Scott Moncrieff, George, *The Mirror and the Cross – Scotland and the Catholic Reformation* (London, 1960)

Stevenson, David, *Scotland's Last Royal Wedding – The Marriage of James VI and Anne of Denmark* (Edinburgh, 1997)

Stewart, Alan, *The Cradle King* (London, 2003)

The Holy Bible: King James Version (Oxford)

Notes

Most of the events and characters in this book are based on real historical figures, and real events. There are two main characters who are not: Lady Marjorie Boswell, a mover and a shaker, and Luca von Modrich, Bohemian ambassador to the court of James 1, although there was a Bohemian ambassador who fulfilled his function at the court and did go on to be instrumental in starting the Thirty Years War.

Dramatis Personae
The characters in italics are fictional

George Heriot – Jeweller to James VI of Scotland
Queen Anna – Queen consort to James VI, daughter of
Frederick II King of Denmark
King James VI of Scotland and I of England
Queen Elizabeth I of England
Mary Queen of Scots – mother of James VI
Lord Darnley – father of James VI
Christian Heriot – wife of George Heriot
Lady Marjorie Boswell – *a Scots noblewoman*
Peter – *Marjorie's brother*
Calum – *Marjorie's brother*

King Frederick II of Denmark – father of Anna

Tygore Delson – *Danish theologian at the Court of Frederick II of Denmark*

Margaret – Danish maid to Queen Anna

Old Mrs Heriot – George Heriot's mother

James – *son of Lady Marjorie*

David Brown – *a neighbour to George*

Lord Lennox – a Scots nobleman

Prince Henry – son of King James and Queen Anna

Don d'Aragno – *Spanish ambassador to the Scottish Court*

Earl and Countess of Mar – Scots nobles charged with the upbringing of princes

Riccio – favourite of Mary Queen of Scots, murdered

Mary – *maid to the Heriots*

Lord Bothwell – Scots nobleman, at one time married to Mary Queen of Scots

Ruth – *Laundry maid at Holyrood Palace*

Jessie – *neighbour to George*

Princess Elizabeth – second child to James and Anna

Princess Margaret – daughter of James and Anna

Prince Charles – fourth child and second son of James and Anna

Lord Melville – Scots nobleman

Lord Huntly – Scots nobleman

Lady Huntly – gentlewoman to the Queen

Maitland, Lennox, Bathgate, Clifford – Scots Lords

Lady Drummond – gentlewoman to the Queen

Sophie of Mecklenburg-Grustow – Queen of Denmark-mother of Queen Anna

William Drummond of Hawthornden – Scots nobleman and poet

Lord Douglas – Scots nobleman

Lord Carey – English nobleman

Lord Fyvie – Scots nobleman

Robert Cecil – English nobleman who becomes Chancellor to the King

Lord Leslie – Scots nobleman

Rachel – *servant to the Heriots in London*

Lord Northampton – English nobleman

Mr Buchanan – *Scots academic*

Lord Pembroke – English nobleman

Fool – *fool at the English court*

Lord Southampton – English nobleman

Lord Buckingham – Scots nobleman given an English title, favourite of James I

William Shakespeare – playwright at the English Court

Inigo Jones – designer of Masques at the English Court, later an architect

Ben Jonson – playwright at the English Court

King Christian IV – King of Denmark, Anna's brother

Bishop of Oxford

Andrew Melville – Scots theologian

Clemence – *a kitchen maid*

Alison – Heriot's second wife

Grizel – Heriot's cousin

Frederick Elector Palatine – husband to Princess Elizabeth, later King and Queen of Bohemia

Douglas – *servant to William of Hawthornden*

Mary – *a poor woman at Hawthornden*

Johnnie – *child of Mary*

Sir Walter Raleigh – English nobleman

Luca von Modrich – *ambassador from Bohemia at the English Court*

Gondomar – Spanish ambassador

Liza – daughter of George Heriot

Clarissa – *lover of Luca von Modrich*

Walter Bancanquall – Heriot's executor

Children of King James and Queen Anna

1. **Henry, Prince of Wales** (19 February 1594 – 6 November 1612). Died, probably of typhoid fever, aged 18.

2. **Elizabeth** (19 August 1596 – 13 February 1662). Married 1613, Frederick V, Elector Palatine. Died aged 65.

3. **Margaret** (24 December 1598 – March 1600). Died aged 1.

4. **Charles I** (19 November 1600 – 30 January 1649). Married 1625, Henrietta Maria. Succeeded James I. Executed aged 48.

5. **Robert**, Duke of Kintyre (18 January 1602 – 27 May

1602). Died aged 4 months.

6. **Mary** (8 April 1605 – 16 December 1607). Died aged 2.

7. **Sophia** (June 1607). Died within 48 hours of birth.